HOT CHOCOLATE AND HOMICIDE

A CHOCOLATE CENTERED COZY MYSTERY

CINDY BELL

CONTENTS

*S*oft music played through the speakers situated throughout the shop, hidden behind an assortment of wooden toys that lined the shelves. It was mood music, according to Charlotte, love songs to get people in the spirit of Valentine's Day.

All Ally knew was that she enjoyed it. With chocolate melting, and candies cooling, she'd been busy all morning, as had her grandmother who tried to keep up with packing the candies into boxes. As soon as she began to feel a little tired a song she enjoyed came on, and she found herself wiggling her hips and humming along.

"It is nice to have such good music playing." Ally carried another tray of chocolates in their molds over to the refrigerator. "Do you think we'll have enough for today?"

"Maybe." Charlotte's brows were knitted as she counted the boxes she'd already put together. "Valentine's Day is one of those holidays that is hard to predict. We'll be busy, but how busy is up in the air."

"I think with the new gift package we're offering we'll be very busy." Ally smiled as she added some mint flavoring to the chocolate she'd melted. "It was such a good idea."

"I agree. I think that being able to create custom hot chocolate to complement the candy that people buy is the perfect way to lead people to a romantic night by the fire. And the temperatures outside make it even more perfect." She turned back to face her granddaughter with a warm smile. "Honestly, even I'm starting to get into the mood to celebrate Valentine's Day, and that hasn't happened in decades."

"Oh really?" She grinned as she met her grandmother's eyes. "What kind of plans do you have, Mee-Maw?"

"Well." She wiped her hands on a towel and walked over to supervise the melted chocolate. "Jeff keeps mentioning how he is going to surprise me, and give me a great Valentine's Day. Honestly, at first I was a little apprehensive. I have been single for so long I am not used to celebrating Valentine's Day." She brushed her long, gray hair back behind her shoulders and tied it once more with a hair tie. "But, he's so excited when he talks about it, now I'm rather curious."

"Oh, Mee-Maw you should just relax and enjoy it. It's so nice that you get to celebrate this Valentine's Day, and you'll always remember your first one with him."

"My first one." She raised an eyebrow. "It might be my last you know."

"Why would you say that?" Ally looked over at her with concern.

"I just mean that we're barely more than friends. I'm not sure that this is going to turn into a long-term relationship, and I'm not sure that I want it to." She washed her hands, then walked over to the refrigerator to retrieve more chocolates to pack.

"The future can be hard to predict." Ally poured chocolate into a new set of molds. They were in the shapes of hearts, arrows, and lips. She thought the lips were a little strange, but the set had been quite popular the year before. "The important thing is that you enjoy yourself now. Just relax and have some fun with him. The rest will fall into place on its own, whether you like it or not."

"Oh really?" She grinned. "Not if I have anything to say about it."

"You won't." Ally's eyes sparkled. "Like you always tell me, love doesn't care about your opinion."

"Love is a strong word." Charlotte's expression softened. "I've only used it once before."

"I know, Mee-Maw." She finished pouring the chocolate and met her grandmother in the center of the kitchen to give her a warm hug. "I know you must still miss him."

"I do." She returned the hug with a subtle squeeze. "Even though I didn't have him long, he left quite an impression on me." She blinked back a few tears then took a deep breath. "What about you? I'm sure Luke has something special planned."

"Hmm. I wouldn't be so sure about that." She cast her gaze around the kitchen in search of another mold to use. Charlotte's Chocolate Heaven was packed with an assortment of molds, and though only a few were meant to be used for Valentine's Day, Ally was always looking for a new combination to surprise their customers with. Her grandmother had handed the reins of the shop over to her, though she still liked to help out in the shop. She'd been very supportive of Ally's new ideas.

"Why is that?" Charlotte looked over at her. "He seems like the romantic type."

"He is." She bit into her bottom lip. "Most of the time. Honestly, it's not his fault. He has to work a long shift that day, so most likely we won't even see each other. I know how important his work is, and I know it's not fair of me to want him all to myself, but I guess being in the middle of all of this makes me more sensitive." She gestured to the molds that covered the table beside her.

"I'm sorry to hear that, Ally, I hope he'll be able to spare a little time for you that day. But you're right, his job is very important. A detective never truly gets a day off." She stacked up some boxes to take to the front of the store.

"I know, and we can always make plans at another time to celebrate. Which will be just as sweet." She smiled. "Really, I'm just lucky to have him in my life at all, he's such a good guy."

"Yes, he is," Charlotte agreed. It had taken her a little time to warm up to Luke Elm. He had struck her as so serious and by the book. But as he and Ally grew closer she discovered that he was a trustworthy man, determined to find justice for those who needed it.

As they stepped into the front of the shop, Ally walked to the front door and unlocked it. She flipped the sign over to open. The moment she did, the door swung open, and Mrs. Bing, Mrs. Cale, and Mrs. White stepped inside. The three senior ladies were regular customers of the shop, and friends of her grandmother. Ally had grown up with them, and all three were like family to her.

"Morning ladies." Ally smiled at them as they hurried to the counter to sample the chocolates that Charlotte had already filled the sample tray with.

"Good morning! So glad we got here before the crowds today." Mrs. White rolled her eyes as she fanned her chest. "Yesterday, it was so crowded that I found it hard to breathe in here."

"Yes, we were quite busy." Charlotte smiled at her as she pushed the sample tray closer to her.

"All of this over a silly holiday." Mrs. Cale rolled her eyes. "Valentine's Day, what poppycock."

"Poppycock?" Mrs. Bing gasped. "Love could never be poppycock."

"It's certainly not something to be celebrated with candy and flowers." Mrs. White lifted her chin with a sniff. "Kids today, know nothing about true romance."

"Hey, don't knock the candy." Ally grinned as she walked over to join them. "We want people to buy them, remember?"

"Oh, don't listen to them." Mrs. Bing waved her hand through the air. "They're just upset because they don't have dates to the Valentine's Day Dance at Freely Lakes. I on the other hand, do, and I can't wait to celebrate." She smiled sweetly at the other two.

"I wouldn't go to that anyway!" Mrs. Cale huffed.

"You would, too." Mrs. White elbowed her lightly. The three settled down a bit as they savored the flavors of the chocolates on the sample tray.

"What is that amazing smell?" Mrs. Bing sniffed the air.

"Ah, that's part of our new gift package." Ally pointed to a carafe on the back counter. "We don't just have coffee to pair with the candy, we have hot chocolate, too. And the best part is we can flavor it to match any of the candies you like. Want a caramel cream hot chocolate?" She knew that was one of Mrs. Bing's favorites, although most of the chocolates were.

"Absolutely!" She clapped her hands with excitement. Soon, all three of the women were set up with a sample of the hot chocolate. Ally had asked her grandmother why the three friends rarely paid for chocolate. Her grandmother explained that one, they were like family, and two, they were the best word of mouth advertisement that she could ever invest in. And she was right. Everywhere the three women went they would speak glowingly about the chocolate shop. They'd had people come to the shop from states away, due to their recommendations.

"Oh, this is so delicious." Mrs. Bing smacked her lips. "I'm definitely sending Carlo in here to get this for me."

"Carlo, Carlo, Carlo." Mrs. White rolled her eyes. "You don't hear Charlotte going on and on about Jeff, do you?"

Charlotte froze. "What about Jeff?"

"Oh, everyone knows that you two are a serious item." Mrs. Cale winked. "Such a cute couple. Are you going to the dance?"

"No, I don't think so." Charlotte blushed slightly. She wasn't used to feeling embarrassed and was relieved when the front door opened and a tall man in a uniform wheeled in a few crates. She hoped he would be the distraction she needed to change the subject.

"Hi, Isaac." Charlotte smiled at him as he rolled the cart further into the shop. "Right on time, as always."

"Morning Charlotte, Ally." He nodded to them both with a warm smile. Then he shifted his gaze in the direction of the three ladies gathered close to the counter. "Mrs. Bing, Mrs. Cale, Mrs. White." He tipped the blue cap he wore. "Good morning, to you all."

"Thank you, Isaac." Mrs. White fixed her gaze on him. "How are things at Bloomdale?"

"Oh fine, fine as they can be." He cleared his throat, then began to unload the crates from the cart. "Should I just put these in the refrigerator for you, Ally?" He glanced over at her.

"That would be great, thank you." She nodded. She noticed that his hair had a bit more gray in it than it used to. He was in his late fifties, and quite fit for his age. She rarely remembered that he was actually older than her, as he lugged heavy crates and made deliveries from dawn until late in the afternoon. "And how is Mrs. Bloomdale?"

"She's well." He carried the crates into the kitchen. Ally walked in front of him to hold open the door for him. As soon as he disappeared through the door, the three women in front of the counter exchanged knowing glances. Charlotte noticed them, but she didn't think too much about it. She was used to the gossip that spread between the three. They always knew about everything that happened in town, and some things that didn't actually happen, but they would swear did. As she sorted through more chocolates to add to the sample tray, Isaac stepped back out into the shop.

"Oh Charlotte, these candies look delicious." He smiled as he eyed them.

"Please, try one." She offered him the tray.

"No, thank you." He waved his hand. "I already know how good they taste. I'd like two boxes please." He studied the boxes on the shelf behind the counter. "Almonds and toffee, and cherry cordials."

"Coming right up. Did you want the hot chocolates to pair with them?" She smiled. "It's a new gift pack we're offering. The hot chocolate will have a similar flavor to the candy. Or, of course, you could choose any other flavor you might like."

"You have one that will taste like cherry cordial?" His eyes widened. "Sure, I'll take that. For both of them, I mean."

"Just be sure to keep the container in the fridge until you're ready to heat it, as it's made with real milk. It has the date on it and instructions on how to heat it." Charlotte put together two small gift baskets with all of the speed and experience of working in the gift business for years. When she slid them over to him, she could see the light in his eyes.

"This is great. Thanks." He pulled out some cash as she rung the transaction up. Once the money and gift baskets had been exchanged he grabbed his cart and began to wheel it to the door. "Goodbye, ladies." He eyed them with a slight smile before he backed out through the door. Ally stepped out of the kitchen just in time to wave to him before he disappeared through the door.

"Did he have gift baskets?" She smiled at her grandmother.

"Yes, he bought the hot chocolate, too. Cherry cordial, and almond and toffee. This could really be an amazing thing for the shop. It's such a unique gift, Ally. You came up with a really great idea." Charlotte gave her a quick pat on her shoulder.

"I thought of it when I was putting together some breakfast for Luke. It was so cold out I wanted to send him with some hot chocolate, and I always pack him a few candies. I realized it was the perfect combination, and that it would be so much fun to customize the hot chocolate."

"It really is clever." Mrs. White nodded as she plucked another chocolate from the sample tray.

"You two just keep inventing new ways to encourage my round physique." Mrs. Bing patted her stomach.

"Better watch it, remember what the doctor said." Mrs. Cale narrowed her eyes.

"Doctor, shmoctor." Mrs. Bing rolled her eyes. "Carlo thinks I'm lovely."

"You are lovely." Ally smiled at her.

"But you should listen to the doctor." Charlotte wagged her finger. "We're not getting any younger, and these bodies don't bounce back like the young-sters." She glanced at Ally. "This one can eat a few pounds of chocolate and never put on a pound of weight."

"Mee-Maw!" Ally laughed. "That isn't true."

"Sure, sure." Charlotte waved her hand. "I'm just glad Isaac bought the gift sets. I'm sure he won't be the last."

"Oh, it's so sad what's going on at that dairy farm." Mrs. Cale sighed.

"What do you mean?" Charlotte rested her

elbows on the counter and leaned forward. "Is something wrong at Bloomdale?"

"Yes, there are big wigs from some giant corporation trying to buy the farm. I heard about it from Laura, and Patti confirmed it." Mrs. Cale pursed her lips. "It's that son-in-law of hers, you know. Gladys Bloomdale would never sell that farm. It's been in her family for generations. But you know how the young people treat us old ladies." She frowned.

"Hey, that's not true." Ally met her eyes.

"It may not be true of you, Ally, but to many we're past our prime, and our opinions matter less and less with every year older we get." Mrs. White folded her arms across her chest. "It's not right, but Mrs. Cale isn't wrong."

"I'm sorry to hear that you experience that." Ally pursed her lips. It always bothered her when anyone treated her grandmother as if she wasn't fully capable of doing whatever she pleased. But she was also guilty at times, of being overprotective of her. To be fair, her grandmother was far more overprotective of Ally. After Ally's mother had passed away, she'd clung to her grandmother a bit more tightly, grateful to have her, and always a little fearful that she might lose her.

"So you think the son-in-law is trying to weasel

the farm out from under her?" Charlotte raised an eyebrow. "I can't see Gladys falling for that. She's sharp."

"Yes, she is, or at least she used to be." Mrs. Bing piped up. "But I've been hearing rumors about her starting to lose her focus. Making silly mistakes. One person said she was even wandering the farm at night."

"See, that's part of the problem right there." Mrs. White put her hands on her hips as she looked at Mrs. Bing. "You shouldn't be repeating things like that. Gladys is as healthy as a horse, and so is her mind."

"I'm sorry!" Mrs. Bing held up her hands. "I didn't say it was true, it's just what I've heard." She shrugged. "Of course, I could be wrong."

"You are wrong." Mrs. White's cheeks flared bright red. "She's a brilliant woman. Do you know she took over that farm when she was only nineteen years old? Her father died suddenly, and her older brother wasn't interested, so it fell on her to keep that farm going. Back then, the thought of a woman, a young girl at that, taking over a farm was unheard of, she was treated very poorly. But she did it! She's a remarkable woman, and I'll not hear another word about her losing her faculties."

"I didn't exactly say that," Mrs. Bing mumbled.

"She is an amazing woman." Mrs. Cale smiled and patted both of their shoulders. "Let's settle down now, all right? It's not helping anything to squabble."

"You're right, you're right." Mrs. White frowned. "I just hate to see someone trying to take advantage of her. And you know, Bernice does nothing about it. She just lets her husband do whatever he pleases. I mean really, what does a mechanic know about running a dairy farm? Nothing! Which is why he wants to sell it. Could you imagine a big corporate type of farm taking over that area?" She clucked her tongue.

"That would be difficult to look at." Charlotte shook her head. "I love our little town."

"But I suppose it's inevitable." Ally rested her hands on the counter as she gazed at the women. "If her daughter and son-in-law don't want to run it, it will be sold eventually."

"Maybe." Mrs. White nodded. "But I'm sure she's not ready to give it up. It's as if some people just stamp an expiry date on us. We get to live the lives we choose, for this long and that's it." She sighed. "One day you'll understand, Ally."

Ally offered her a sympathetic smile, but her

stomach churned. She hoped that wasn't the case. But she did see Mrs. White's point. It was common-place for older people to be spoken down to, or treated as if they weren't modern enough to have an opinion. Luckily for her, she considered her grand-mother her best friend, and had always valued her opinion above anyone else's.

"Well, it's nothing to worry about now. If she refuses to sell, then there's nothing that her son-in-law can do about it, right?" Ally shrugged.

"Maybe." Mrs. White's brows knitted so tight that a deep wrinkle appeared across her forehead. Ally could tell that she was very concerned. As the three ladies left the shop Ally took a moment to give her grandmother a tight hug.

"What was that for?" Charlotte laughed.

"I just want you to know how grateful I am for you."

"Oh, Ally don't listen to them. You only get old if you let yourself, and there's one thing I can assure you of, Gladys Bloomdale will never get old."

CHAPTER 2

*A*fter another steady rush, Ally was exhausted. She looked over at her grand-mother as the last customer stepped out the door.

"Are you sure you're going to be able to handle this on your own while I'm at lunch with Luke?"

"Of course, I'm sure." She winked at her. "Remember, I have a lot more experience at this than you."

"Yes, I know. I really appreciate you covering for me so I can spend some time with him. He's so busy it's hard to get any quality time in with him. I want to make sure we get some face to face. Other-wise he might forget about me." She frowned as she pulled off her apron. "He was supposed to be here ten minutes ago."

"Ally, you're not serious about that, are you?"

Charlotte wiped down the counter, then started to refill the sample trays. "You know he is mad about you, right?"

"I'm not sure about that." She smiled, despite her concern. "And no I guess I'm not entirely serious about it. I keep telling myself how important his job is, and how he's helping people, and protecting our community. But it's hard not to wonder if he's just tired of spending time with me when he can't even manage to show up for lunch on time." She glanced at the clock again. "Or maybe he's not going to show up at all."

"Maybe you should text him and remind him?" Charlotte frowned. "Men aren't always good at keeping up with commitments. He could have gotten busy with a case and forgot that he had plans. That doesn't mean that he's forgetting you." She reached out and rubbed her shoulder. "You're a beautiful woman, Ally, and Luke knows how wonderful you are. I really don't think that he means any harm by being so busy."

"I know you're right." She pulled out her phone. "Honestly, I think I wanted him to remember on his own, but I guess that's not fair of me. He is very busy." She typed out a text and sent it through. A second later she heard a buzz that didn't come from her phone. She looked up to see Luke walk through the door. His face was red and he looked a bit stressed out.

"Ally, I'm so sorry." He pulled out his phone as he walked towards her, then looked down at the text. "Oh sweetheart, I could never forget about you." He pulled her close and they shared a lingering kiss. When they broke apart, he stared into her eyes. "Do you forgive me?"

"Nothing to forgive." She looked into his tired eyes. She could tell that he had been working hard. "Do you still have time for lunch?"

"Yes." He glanced over at Charlotte. "How are you today?"

"Very well, thank you." She winked at him. "You two get out of here while you can. I can hold down the fort."

"Thank you, Mee-Maw." She blew her grand-mother a kiss as Luke led her out of the shop. Normally, they would walk down to the diner at the end of the street, but with so little time left for lunch, Luke offered to drive. As they drove down the street, Ally savored their closeness in the car. She loved spending time with him.

Luckily, the diner was not very crowded. They

were able to get their usual table. As they settled in, she looked across the table at him with a smile.

"The new candy and hot chocolate combination is doing very well."

"I'm glad to hear it. It's such a good idea. I'm going to get some for you, you know."

"You are?" She laughed. "What flavor?"

"I haven't decided yet. All I know is that I want to feed you candy by the fire." He slipped his hand around hers. "How does that sound to you?"

"It sounds wonderful." She sighed as the warmth of his touch made all of the tension leave her body. "Maybe on Monday night?"

"Right." His lips tensed. "I know, I have to work late on Valentine's Day. Monday would be good. But, I'm going to try to work it so that I can at least try to take you out to dinner. It just might be a last-minute kind of thing. You're not going to have any other dates, are you?" He raised an eyebrow.

"Not a chance." She grinned. "But I might commit a crime just so I can see you." She glanced around the diner. "Would you show up if I robbed the diner?"

"Funny." He leveled his gaze on hers. "No getting arrested. Got it?"

"Got it." She laughed. "If you can get some free

time that's great, but you don't have to stress about it, Luke."

"Thank you." He smiled at her and trailed his hand across hers. "I know you understand, but I still hate not being able to be there with you on a special day."

"Any day we spend together is a special day. It's no big deal." She sat back as the waitress arrived to take their orders. Once they'd been placed, Luke edged his chair closer to hers. She could tell that he was really trying to be there with her, but the look in his eyes informed her that he had something on his mind.

"Are you working a difficult case?"

"Just finished one." He lowered his eyes. "I didn't think it would ever end, and now that it has, honestly I wish it had turned out differently. Sometimes it's hard to remember that there are many good people in the world. But then I see you." He smiled as he looked back up into her eyes. "And you remind me that there is so much beauty, so much goodness."

She blushed as she glanced away from him. He could be very romantic when he wanted to be, despite his usual focus on logic.

"I'm glad I can do that for you." She squeezed

his hand. Just as they were about to lean close and kiss, his cell phone buzzed. He ignored it at first and leaned closer to her lips, then it buzzed again. She sat back and smiled. "You should probably check that."

As he reached for his phone, it began to ring. His expression grew more serious as he recognized the name on the screen.

"Yes, Chief?" He placed the phone against his ear. His expression grew more grim as he nodded. "All right, I'll be right there. Yes, maybe ten minutes. Okay then. Right." He hung up the phone and stared across the table at Ally. "I am so, so sorry."

"It's all right." She smiled. "Don't worry about it. I know it must be important."

"It is." He frowned. "I have to run. Let me take you back to the shop." He stood up from the table.

"No, don't worry about that. I can walk. You just go." Her heart began to pound. She knew that if he had to leave lunch, then it must be serious. "Check in with me when you can."

"I will." He stole one more kiss from her, his lips barely grazing hers, then bolted out the diner. As she waited for their lunch to be delivered, she wondered what the case might be about. The waitress had already boxed up their food for them. It wasn't the first time that Luke had to run out on a meal.

"Everything okay, Ally?" She handed her the meals as Ally handed her money to cover it as well as a tip.

"Something big must have happened for him to take off like that." Ally shook her head. "I don't know what, though. I'm sure we'll all know soon enough."

~

On her walk back to the shop, Ally began to notice people clustering together. It was chilly enough that there weren't many people outside, but those that were, had gathered close to one another. She wondered why, but kept her focus on getting to the shop. She shivered as a cool breeze carried across her cheeks. The colder it got, the more she wondered whether winter would ever end. She looked forward to the spring weather that would bring about picnics in the park and hopefully many sunny days. She was soon at the front of the shop. When she glanced back over her shoulder she noticed that even more people had gathered together. Clearly, they had something to discuss. She pulled open the door of the shop and stepped inside. It was empty of customers, but the moment that her grandmother spotted her, she rounded the counter and walked over to her.

"Ally, have you heard?" She fixed her granddaughter with a worried gaze.

"Heard what?" She frowned. "Luke had to take off from our lunch because something happened, but I don't know what. Is it already news around town?"

"Yes, the last person who was in here told me about it. You're not going to believe this. Gladys Bloomdale is dead." She took her granddaughter's hands and looked into her eyes. "They found her not long after you left here."

"Dead?" Her eyes widened. "How strange, when we were just talking about her. Was it some kind of accident?" She frowned.

"Yes, a terrible accident. She crashed a quad bike on the way back to the house on the farm. She must have been going terribly fast." She sighed. "I've never known Gladys to be so reckless. But I guess, sometimes it happens. We all get a little distracted, or stressed, and make poor choices."

"Didn't she have a helmet?" Ally swallowed hard

as she thought of the woman. She didn't know her well, but she hated to think of her dying.

"I don't know any details about it, but maybe not. I think sometimes people get used to driving around on their own property and probably don't take proper precautions. I'm not sure." She sighed. "And really, it doesn't matter now. All that matters is that she is gone."

"Oh, Mee-Maw I'm sorry." She hugged her grandmother tight. "I know she was a friend of yours."

"Not quite a friend, not exactly, but it's always hard to lose someone who has been part of the community for so very long." She shook her head. "All I can think of is Bernice. She's still so young, with children of her own."

"Yes, that is very hard." Ally lowered her eyes as her own grief for the loss of her mother when she was so young, rose up through her. She brushed it away and looked into her grandmother's eyes again. "Why don't you go on home for the day? I can close up here."

"No, it's okay." She smiled and patted her grand-daughter's cheek. "We're about to get a rush." She tipped her head towards a group of people that were just arriving outside of the shop.

As the customers entered the shop Ally did her best to greet them with a friendly smile. However, she didn't feel cheerful. She thought about the tragedy. At least it was just an accident, which would make Luke's involvement in it short. After the rush had died down and everyone had left, two locals stepped in. Ally knew their faces, but not their names. They grazed the sample chocolates, and immediately brought up the subject of Gladys' death.

"She never should have been on that quad bike." The middle-aged woman shook her head. "She was too old to be on something like that."

"Nonsense." The younger woman beside her eyed her with annoyance. "Gladys was always on the quad bike. She's been riding that thing around the farm for decades. There was no reason for her not to be on it."

"Clearly there was, otherwise she wouldn't be dead." The older woman snorted.

"Ladies." Charlotte interrupted the conversation. "Would you like to try some hot chocolate?"

"No thanks." The younger woman smiled. "But I do want a box of mocha truffles."

"Coming right up." Charlotte smiled in return.

"And I'll take some raspberry creams, please." The older woman nodded to Ally.

"Absolutely." Ally packed them up. She hoped the conversation about Gladys would come to an end. However, the older woman seemed determined to continue it.

"You know she wasn't what she used to be. She'd gotten a little confused in her old age. Once she was wandering the farm and the police had to be called to find her."

"That's not what happened." The younger woman narrowed her eyes. "She didn't want to be found. It was her meddling son-in-law that was determined she be brought back to the house. She could have lived off the land on that farm for as long as she pleased. But he told the police she was lost, when she was really just mad."

"So says you." She rolled her eyes.

"So said Gladys. She let those police have it." She laughed at the memory. "Heaven forbid one of them ever tread on her property again without permission." Her smile faded, then she grimaced. "I guess that's not the case anymore."

"Well, whatever happened, I'm sure we will find out more as the days go on." Ally walked both women to the door. "Thank you for coming in." Once she'd closed the door behind them, she looked back at her grandmother. "It's interesting how everyone seems to know everything at this point. What it comes down to, is that there was a terrible accident that led to a tragedy, and that's bad enough without arguing about it."

"That's true." Charlotte glanced up towards the door as Luke swung it open. "It looks like we might find out a little more."

CHAPTER 3

*a*lly and Charlotte looked at Luke as he stepped into the shop. Ally noticed right away that his hazel eyes were exhausted. His hair was ruffled, and his shirt was wrinkled. It looked like he had aged years in the time since she'd seen him at lunch.

"Luke." Ally smiled as he walked towards her.

"Ally, I'm sorry I had to walk out on lunch today." He paused in front of her. "It was an emergency."

"I know it was. Don't worry about that. Are you okay?" She wrapped an arm around his shoulders. "I know it must have been tough for you, it was such a tragic accident."

"It was difficult." He grimaced and turned in

closer to her. He glanced towards the door. "Are you closing up?"

"Yes, I was just about to lock up." She pulled away from him and walked towards the door.

"Good idea." He ran his hand back through his hair. "I want to tell you something, but it can't go further than this shop." He looked over at Charlotte, then back at Ally. "News about it will get around soon enough, but I would prefer if you keep it quiet for now."

"What is it?" Ally walked back over to him, her eyes wide as her heart skipped a beat. If Luke was being this careful about it she guessed that it was something very serious. As much as she wanted to know, she was also a little afraid to find out.

"It wasn't an accident." He frowned as he looked into her eyes. "It looked like an accident, but it wasn't."

"Are you certain?" Charlotte walked over to join them, the color faded from her skin. "Then what was it?"

"It looked like she'd run the quad into a shed at a very high speed. Of course questions were raised. Why would she drive straight into the shed like that? Why didn't she apply the brakes? After some investigation we discovered that the brake lines for the quad were cut. She probably lost control on the hill that led to the shed and was unable to slow herself down." He rubbed the heel of his palm along the ridge of one eye. "Now the question of course, is who would kill her?" When he opened his eyes again, they were bleary and tinged red.

"That's terrible." Ally looked over at her grand-mother, who grasped on to her shoulder to steady herself. "Are you okay, Mee-Maw?"

"I don't think so." She shivered. Ally could feel it in the fingers that held on to her. "How could this happen to Gladys?"

"That's what I intend to find out." He blinked a few times, then turned his attention back to Ally. "I just wanted to stop in and apologize about lunch again. I hate having to walk out on you like that."

"Sweetie, you don't need to apologize, but you do need some sleep." She caressed his cheek. "When was the last time you were home for a full night's sleep?"

"Uh, I'm not really sure. I've grabbed a few naps here and there. I'll be fine, I promise." He touched his lips to hers in a light kiss. "I've got to get back to the station to go over some witness statements. Now that it's been declared a homicide we'll have to go back over everything."

"Luke really, they can spare you for a few hours. Get some rest." She took his hands in hers, tempted to ask him to stay. "I worry about you working this hard."

"I know." He rested his head against hers for a moment. "But the first twenty-four hours of a murder investigation are crucial. I can't miss any of them. Any chance you have any coffee left?"

"Sure." Charlotte smiled as she stepped back around the counter. "I'll make you up a thermos to take with you."

While she busied herself preparing the thermos, Ally focused in on Luke. She wanted to be supportive, but she also wanted him to be healthy, and she could tell from the exhaustion in his expression that he was pushing himself far too hard.

"Do you have any leads, yet? Anything promising? What about the son-in-law?"

"I can't really talk about that." He furrowed a brow. "What do you know about the son-in-law?"

"Nothing really, just some rumors that were flying through here earlier. Nothing concrete." She frowned. "I wish I knew so you could solve this and get some rest."

"I hope that it goes fast. Not just for my sake, but for her family's. She has a daughter, and grandchildren, but apparently the farm workers on the property are also like a second family to her. Many of them have been working there for years. Of course, what makes things a little more complicated is that she had a tendency to hire ex-cons."

"What?" Ally's voice rose with surprise. "I had no idea she did that."

"Yes." Luke nodded as Charlotte returned to them with a thermos of coffee for him. "She spear-headed a few charitable programs for people transitioning from prison. They didn't take off very well around here. I don't know that much about her, but I do know that she had a special passion for reformed criminals."

"Reformed?" Ally swallowed hard. "What if one of them wasn't so reformed?"

"That's what I have to figure out." He took the thermos from Charlotte. "Thanks so much for this. I really appreciate it."

"Anytime, Luke, you know that." Charlotte patted his shoulder, her eyes lingered on his for a moment. "I'm proud of you, you know. You work very hard out there each day. I already know you'll do your best on this case, but I feel I should warn you, since you didn't grow up here, this kind of case is going to be very difficult. People will all have an opinion about it. Gladys lived here so long that she wasn't just a resident, she was a part of the town itself, and everyone will think they can claim owner-ship of her somehow. Just keep in mind that tongues wag faster than a hummingbird's wings in a small town, and not all of them spout accurate information."

"Thanks for the warning, Charlotte. I'll keep it in mind. And thanks again for the coffee." He kissed Ally on the cheek, then turned towards the door.

"Be careful, Luke." Ally watched him step out through the door. He glanced back and gave her a light wink. She wanted to be reassured by it, but she wasn't. As she walked back to the door and locked it, she had to fight the urge to stop him from leaving. Something about the investigation already had her on edge, but she didn't know what just yet. When she turned back to her grandmother, she found her standing in the middle of the shop, her eyes dazed and lips slightly parted.

"Mee-Maw? Are you okay?" She walked over to her and slipped her arms around her.

"You know, I was right." She rested her head against Ally's,

"About what?" She stroked her grandmother's hair.

"Gladys will never get old. She'll never have the chance. It's just hard to imagine someone as strong as that, simply being gone. And to find out that someone did this to her, that it wasn't just some freak accident that nothing could explain, it just makes it that much harder to endure."

"You're right, Mee-Maw." She closed her eyes for a moment. "She will be missed by the whole town."

"And especially her daughter, Bernice." She pulled away from Ally and headed towards the kitchen. "I'm going to put together some chocolates to take to her tomorrow. It's best that we take the time to visit her and express our condolences."

"Good idea." Ally watched her grandmother until she disappeared into the kitchen, then set about cleaning up the rest of the shop. In all of the chaos and Valentine's Day excitement, she'd lost track of what really mattered. She still had the people she loved. Not everyone was going to be so lucky this holiday. As she closed down the cash register she considered what might have happened to Gladys. Obviously, someone wanted her dead. The only possibility that she could think of was the big corporation that wanted to buy her farm. She'd heard of companies bullying people through financial pressure, and other legal means, but would a company really go so far as to eliminate the owner of a small dairy farm?

Ally was still lost in thought when she stepped out to the back of the shop to put out the trash. In the dim light of the evening the eaves of surrounding buildings cast long shadows against the pavement. She barely noticed them as she carried the bag of trash to the dumpster. It wasn't until one of those shadows moved that something in the back of her mind recognized there was no logical explanation for the shadow of an inanimate object to be moving. She spun on her heel, just as a man stepped up behind her. She raised her hands in front of her face, ready to defend and strike in the same moment.

"S-sorry," the man stuttered. "I didn't mean to s-sneak up on you."

"Who are you?" She lowered her hands just enough to see him. He wasn't an intimidating figure. He had a petite frame, and was thin to the point of appearing frail.

"Marlo," he mumbled his name. "You don't know me. No one around here does." He shifted from one foot to the other. "I never really leave the farm."

"The farm? What farm?" She studied him as her fear continued to diminish. He didn't seem to be there to cause her any harm. "Bloomdale farm?" She locked eyes with him.

"Yes, that's it." He cleared his throat. "Your boyfriend, he's a detective, right?"

"How did you know that?" She folded her arms across her chest.

"Never mind." He cleared his throat again. Then shuffled his feet. "I'm sorry. I didn't mean to scare you." He turned and started to walk away.

"Wait, Marlo! Why do you want to know about Luke?" She took a step towards him, but he broke into a run. Within seconds he had disappeared into the nearby woods. He might appear harmless, but she wasn't about to chase him through the woods in the dark. As she made her way back into the shop, her mind was left unsettled.

CHAPTER 4

When Ally arrived home, she was relieved to be greeted by her two favorite friends. Arnold, a pot-bellied pig who had been her grandmother's pet for many years, and Peaches, her cat, who had been her best friend for as long as she'd had her. Both brought a sense of cheerfulness back into her mind as she crouched down to say hello to them. Arnold snorted into her palm, nuzzling her skin as if he could sense that something was wrong. Peaches wound her way through Ally's leg and rubbed her body against the curve of her knee, also in an attempt to comfort her.

"Yes, it was a difficult day, guys." She sighed as she looked into their eyes. "I'm not sure that tomorrow will be any better." She straightened up and took a step forward. The moment she did, both animals bolted towards the kitchen. Arnold tried to knock Peaches out of the way to get there first, but Peaches jumped up onto a small table near the kitchen door and flung herself into the air to sail right over him. She landed on her feet right next to her food dish as Arnold lumbered in behind her.

"Ah, hungry are you?" Ally grinned. It didn't matter how often she fed them both they were always eager to eat. She thought it was interesting how they could be such different animals with different personalities, but they still had a few things in common. After she filled their dishes, she opened the refrigerator to look at her own choices. Her stomach rumbled with hunger. She realized she had left her lunch at the shop, and hadn't eaten anything more than a few bites of chocolate since breakfast. As she rummaged for something that looked good to her, she wondered how she could be hungry and yet not want to eat anything. In the end she settled on some ice cream and a banana. It wasn't exactly healthy, but traumatic days required emergency comfort food.

Once Ally was on the couch, Peaches jumped up and curled up on a cushion beside her. Arnold sprawled out on the floor by her feet. One of the best parts about coming home to the cottage she'd spent the second half of her childhood in, was that she was never alone. Not only was she surrounded by loving pets, but she was also surrounded by wonderful memories of living with her grandmother. She flipped on the news as she ate her ice cream. Gladys Bloomdale's death was the main story. That didn't surprise her, as even though the town of Blue River was a small one, many of the local farms supplied other nearby towns as well, and so were known throughout the area. The reporter who spoke about Gladys indicated that there had been foul play involved in the woman's death. The camera panned over the farm. It was still daylight, so she guessed the footage had been recorded earlier. It didn't show the damaged quad bike, but did show the area near the shed that was roped off with bright yellow police tape. As she watched, her heart lurched. There was Marlo, not far off from the police tape. He seemed to be staring at someone off camera. When he noticed he was being filmed, he ducked out of view.

Marlo. The name stood out in her mind. Was he one of the ex-cons that Gladys had hired? She guessed that he might be, maybe that was why he was camera shy. What had he wanted when he came to her tonight? Why had he asked about Luke? Her stomach churned as she wondered if she might have been in more danger than she realized. She calmed it with another spoon of ice cream.

As the news shifted to another story she turned the television off and grabbed her laptop. She didn't have to wait until the next day to test out a few theories that were forming in her mind. The most prominent one was the idea that perhaps the corporation interested in buying Gladys' dairy farm had somehow caused her death. Of course, it seemed like a stretch to her that some big and wealthy organization would risk murdering someone just for the sake of business. But that didn't mean it wasn't possible, and so far it was the best lead she had.

Ally did a search on Grainder, the corporation, and discovered that it was heavily invested in dairy production. While she expected it to have other interests, she didn't find too many.

Once she'd been through its website and found out some very general information about the business from its self-promoting content, she shifted gears. Instead of searching for the business, she searched for complaints against the business. It didn't take long to find them. There were hundreds of comments on an assortment of sites. She noticed that many of them came from owners of small businesses. Those owners claimed that they had been forced to sell their companies. Some complained about financial pressure, while others said resources they needed to keep their businesses afloat were cut off or bought off by the larger corporation.

One complaint in particular indicated that physical intimidation had been used, including several visits to his business, as well as his home, and a sense of being followed. She was shocked by that and wondered if it might just be one person who exaggerated his experience with the company. She clicked on a link that led to a site he'd created to try to stand up against the corporation. On this site she found even more stories of physical intimidation, including one person who insisted that a private detective had been hired to investigate her life. She claimed that he was investigating rumors of an affair, but he never found any proof. The allegations had still destroyed her marriage, as well as her company, in the process. She ended up selling to the company for far less than her business was worth as she had no other choice.

Stunned, Ally decided to print out the story. As the printer came to life with clicks and whirring she thought about Gladys speeding on her farm. Was she being followed? Was that why she was going so fast? Maybe the cut brake lines were just an added element that led to the crash. If she thought she had someone to fear, she might have thrown caution to the wind and gone much faster down that hill than she ever had before. She decided she would take the story to Luke the next day. He needed to know exactly what kind of corporation he was dealing with.

As Ally headed to bed for the evening, memories of Marlo popped up in her mind. Marlo. Was he working with the corporation to intimidate Gladys? Or did he know something that he wanted to tell Luke? She hoped she hadn't scared off what might be the only real lead. She decided she would visit the farm the next day and see if she could track down Marlo for another conversation, in the daylight. As she finally closed her eyes and drifted off to sleep, her mind was still unsettled. Now she understood why Luke didn't sleep much while working a case. It was very difficult to shut off the mind once it started spinning.

~

harlotte glanced at the clock. It was nearly midnight. She looked back up at the ceiling. She couldn't fall asleep. She'd been trying since about nine. It was useless to lay in bed and waste hours. She'd already waded through all of her thoughts about Gladys. She couldn't quite figure out why she was taking the woman's death so hard. They weren't close friends. In fact there were many things that she didn't particularly like about Gladys. She was very bossy, demanding, and had very little sympathy for others. She also wasn't fond of children. She remembered a moment that she hoped Ally was too young to recall, when she took her then five-year-old granddaughter to visit the dairy farm. Ally wanted to see the cows, and Charlotte got permission from one of the farm hands to bring her out to visit them. Ally was so excited when she ran up to one of the cows. That was when Gladys swooped in on her quad bike.

"What are you doing here?" She barked at both of them. Ally was a very shy child at the time, and the anger in Gladys' voice made her burst instantly into tears. It was a heartbreaking moment for Charlotte to see her granddaughter go from excitement to fear. She held Ally close against her as she asked Gladys what the problem was, and insisted that she had permission to be there.

"Not from me, you don't." She stepped off the

quad bike. "Did you bring her out here so she could get hurt and you could sue me and take everything I own?" She huffed as she looked between the two of them. "I'm not about to risk my livelihood so you can have a little meet and greet with a cow. Take her to a petting zoo like normal people. I'm sure they'll have a cow you can pet. But don't bring her here."

"I'm sorry. I asked for permission, and was told it was fine."

"Who? Who did you ask for permission?" Gladys' eyes flashed.

In that moment Charlotte realized she was about to get someone fired. So, she did something she rarely did, especially around her granddaughter. She lied.

"No one. I didn't think it would be a big deal. I just brought her out here on my own. I'm sorry, Gladys, it won't happen again."

"Good." She scowled down at Ally. "Take a lesson from this, kid. Don't go onto other people's property, got it? It won't end well for you."

Ally trembled as she clung to her grandmother, her pudgy cheeks stained with tears. Charlotte steered her down the path that led back to their car. Even then, Ally had been smart. She insisted that her grandmother explain why she lied. It was a memory that Charlotte preferred to forget, but now it had come, so vivid. After that moment she tended to try and avoid Gladys. But they were still women, running businesses in a small town, where not many other women had been able to do the same. Now and then they ran into each other at functions, and were always pleasant to each other. But Charlotte could never forget the way the woman scowled at Ally. She was certain that she had very little patience for children. Around town it was known that Bernice, Gladys' daughter was often expected to work long hours on the farm and barely allowed to have a social life. She guessed that it had to be a very difficult life for her.

When Charlotte finally sat up in bed, she decided that sleep wasn't really a possibility. She reached for her phone and found the last text that Jeff sent her.

If you need me, I'll be there. If you want to talk, I'm here.

He'd asked to come over and spend some time with her when he heard the news, but she'd told him she was fine and would rather be alone. Now she wondered if that was the case. She wasn't the type to try to contact someone so late, but he had said he would be available, and she knew that he was a night owl. He was often still up past one in the morning. After taking a deep breath she typed out a text to him.

Can't sleep.

An instant later he responded.

Care for a walk under the stars?

She shivered at the thought of how cold it would be outside. But the idea of sharing that time with Jeff thrilled her. She agreed to the walk, and bundled herself up. Once she was sure she would be warm enough she walked towards the door. When she opened it, Jeff was just arriving. They both lived in Freely Lakes, a retirement community. His apartment was in another building, but it only took a few minutes to walk from one building to the other. He was bundled up, too.

"We look like we're ready for an arctic expedition." He grinned and planted a kiss on her cheek.

"I'm sorry to bother you so late, I just can't seem to get my thoughts to settle down."

"I understand." He looped his arm through hers. "It's never too late to call me, and you're never a bother." He patted her hand through her thick glove, then led her down the hall to one of the rear exits of the building. Freely Lakes was situated on a sprawling piece of property that extended further than the eye could see. It was on the border of Freely and was situated far enough from both towns that there wasn't much light beyond the security lights that spread out from the building itself. Once they'd walked down a path for some time, the sky came alive with vivid stars.

"Oh Jeff." She rested her head against the thick sleeve of his jacket. "This was exactly what I needed. How did you know that?"

"Whenever I can't sleep, I go for a walk. Something about seeing the stars, breathing the fresh air, always brings things into perspective for me. I realize I'm not much more than a speck when I see the stars spread out above me."

"You're much more than a speck to me." She gave his arm a subtle squeeze. "But you're right, it does put things into perspective very well."

"Is it about Gladys?" He glanced at her. "Is that why you can't sleep?"

"It's about a lot of things. Blue River, specifically. It's hard to believe when something tragic happens here. It's always been my safe place. I hate to think that someone plotted against her, and then acted out that plot. Maybe even one of our neighbors, or a customer at the shop."

"It's hard to believe, but these things happen in

all towns, no matter how safe they are. People act out of rage, jealousy, greed. It's not something that stops at any town lines."

"Yes, you're right." She sighed. "But I do wish it would."

"Is Luke working the case?"

"Yes, and poor Ally is so worried about him. I am, too, to be honest. He looks more tired than I've ever seen him. But he loves his job."

"That he does." Jeff smiled some. "But, that's his job. It's not an easy one."

"Much harder than anything I've ever done."

"I wouldn't say that." He grinned. "I can only imagine the madhouse your shop is going to be as Valentine's Day gets closer."

"That's for sure." She smiled. "And I'm sure you're very busy, too, with jewelry orders."

"I've had quite a few." He nodded. "Some pieces are a bit more challenging than others, but every-thing should be ready by Valentine's Day. Speaking of Valentine's Day—"

"I'd rather not." She glanced up at him. "Not right now."

"All right, but I have plans for you. No deciding to cover for Ally, got it?"

She eyed him for a moment. She wondered if she

should inform him that she would always put her granddaughter first, but she knew he was just trying to be sweet and insistent, not controlling.

"I'll do my best." She pressed her icy lips to his. As they kissed, the temperature around them didn't seem to matter. She was warmed by his closeness, and could have stayed in his embrace for the rest of the night. But suddenly she was tired. She knew she could finally sleep. After she said goodnight to Jeff, she crawled into bed, and closed her eyes. As relieved as she was to be able to rest, she knew that the day ahead would be filled with difficult moments.

CHAPTER 5

*T*he next morning when Ally got to the shop, her grandmother hadn't arrived yet. She prepared the shop for opening, and began making some fresh chocolates for the day. As she worked she thought about the information she'd found out about the corporation that was putting pressure on Gladys. After reading the posts about their strong-arm tactics, she was certain that they couldn't be ruled out as causing Gladys' death. She grabbed her phone and dialed Luke's number. He answered on the third ring, his voice a bit more peppy than it had been the day before.

"Morning Ally. How are you?"

"I'm all right. Did you get some sleep?"

"Yes, Chief's orders, he made me camp out in his

office. I'm feeling a little more refreshed. What about you, did you sleep okay?"

"Decent." She shrugged. It wasn't exactly true, but it was true enough. "Listen, I did some research on Grainder, the company that's trying to buy Bloomdale farm. It has a very dark reputation. Have you looked into it?"

"Yes. I've even spoken to a few people who had the most serious complaints. However, I haven't been able to find any actual proof of the claims the victims presented."

"So you can't do anything about it?"

"I'm not sure at this point if anything should be done about it. Sometimes people get angry and make stuff up. You can't just take one person's word."

"No maybe not, but what if it's more than one person?"

"Business can be tough. Some people take it very personally. But without proof of actual harassment or intimidation, there's nothing I can do about it. However, I am meeting with Rick, the representative from Grainder who was due to meet with Gladys. In fact, she was on the way to a meeting with him when the crash happened. So, I'm very curious to hear what he has to say."

"I know you're busy. Be careful, Luke."

"I will, you too. Don't get too involved in this, Ally."

After he hung up the phone she shifted her attention back to the chocolates she was making. Gladys was on her way to a meeting with Rick when she crashed. Was she rushing to get there on time? Was she upset about what the outcome of the meeting might be? She wished there was some way she could get a clear picture of what the woman was feeling and thinking that day.

"Ally?" Charlotte called out as she stepped into the shop. "Are you back there?"

"Yes, Mee-Maw, I'll be right out. You can leave the door unlocked, it's just about time to open."

"Will do."

As she piled some chocolate covered nuts onto the trays to put in the display cabinet, her grandmother stepped into the kitchen.

"I'm sorry I'm late. I had a hard time getting to sleep last night."

"Mee-Maw, you're not late. You can come in whenever you want, you know that. I'm sorry you didn't sleep well." She gave her a warm hug. "I thought last night might be kind of rough for you."

"It was, a bit. I just kept running everything

through my mind." She sighed. "But today is a new day, and there's only one way to move forward from all of this."

"What way is that?" She met her eyes as she picked up two of the trays.

"We need to find out the truth. If we can do that, then we'll be able to put all of this behind us."

"And maybe prevent a criminal company from profiting from her death." Ally pursed her lips. "I hate to think that they will get away with murder and then gain from it."

"You really think it was the company?" Charlotte picked up two other trays and carried them through the door into the front.

"I think it's a definite possibility. Some of the things they've done in the past make me wonder how it can be legal for them to be in business." She slid her trays into the display. "I just can't believe what some people are capable of doing."

"I know it's hard to believe, but you don't know the lives that they lived that led to their actions." Charlotte tilted her head back and forth. "It's easy to judge, not so easy to actually face the truth about a person, no matter how unpleasant it may be."

"I guess you're right about that." She took the

trays from her grandmother and slid them into place.

Not long after they opened the shop, Mrs. Bing, Mrs. Cale, and Mrs. White arrived. This time they had so much to talk about they barely touched the samples. At first.

"The whole town is buzzing," Mrs. Bing gasped. "To think, murder?"

Ally grimaced. She knew that the news would spread quickly, and it sounded like all of the details of the case were being discussed throughout the town. She hoped it wouldn't cause any harm to Luke's case. Too curious not to ask, she leaned a little closer to the women.

"So, what are people talking about?"

"Mostly the family." Mrs. Cale pursed her lips, then rolled her eyes. "What good is family if all they do is turn their backs on you?"

"What do you mean?" Charlotte added a few more candies to the sample tray, which caught Mrs. Bing's attention.

"Oh, I've heard quite a bit about the family life. As it turns out, the farm was experiencing some financial stress." Mrs. Cale shook her head. "I never knew a thing about it. Apparently, Gladys was just barely keeping her head above water. But her son-in-law, Parker, was pushing her to sell the farm."

"That's because his shop is about to go under." Mrs. Bing popped a chocolate in her mouth and nodded. "I heard all about that today."

"Did you?" Mrs. White raised an eyebrow. "From who?"

"Carla, she does Bernice's hair. She said Bernice had to cancel her appointment because she didn't have the money. She even tried to get Carla to cut it for her and promised to pay her after the sale of the farm went through."

"Interesting." Charlotte narrowed her eyes. "Bernice had to know that her mother had no interest in selling that farm. Why would she be so confident in the sale?"

"Good question." Mrs. Cale drew a sharp line across the slope of her neck. "Unless they're the ones who took care of the problem."

"Bite your tongue!" Mrs. White gasped. "That's Gladys' daughter you're talking about. No one could do that to their mother."

"I wouldn't be so sure about that, it's happened before, plenty of times. Maybe she was just tired of waiting for her inheritance." Mrs. Bing shrugged. "No matter what, the truth about

Gladys is starting to come out, and I think it's a shame. She would hate all of these people digging into her life."

"Well, she's not here to complain." Mrs. White frowned. "And I'm sure the police will figure out who did this to her very swiftly."

"Me too." Ally nodded. "The son-in-law is a mechanic, right?"

"Yes, he owns that shop out on highway fifty. Parker's Place or something cutesy like that." Mrs. White narrowed her eyes. "I only take my car to one shop, have for the past forty years, no cutesy name is going to change that."

The three women began to squabble between themselves about which automobile repair shop was the best.

"Look, it's Isaac with the milk." Charlotte breathed a sigh of relief. "We were almost out, and I was a little worried that I'd have to go to the store to buy some. I wonder if the farm is even running today."

"That's a good question. I wanted to stop by there today. Remember, I told you about the guy I ran into at the dumpster last night? Marlo?"

"Yes, I remember." Charlotte frowned. "That was a scary moment. I don't like you going out there at night. From now on we put the trash out in the morning."

"Mee-Maw, it's fine. Anyway, I wanted to see if I could find out a bit more about him, or even talk with him again. So, I thought we could go by the farm after we visit Bernice."

"That's a good idea." Charlotte nodded. She walked over to the door and held it open for Isaac. He rolled his cart through without the sunny smile he usually wore.

"Morning." He cleared his throat.

Ally noticed that his skin looked pale, and his eyes were a bit swollen. He wheeled the cart behind the counter and towards the kitchen.

"I'll just put these in here for you."

Charlotte followed after him while Ally focused on a few customers who had walked in behind Isaac.

"Isaac, are you all right?" Charlotte let the kitchen door swing closed behind them.

"Not exactly." He sniffled as he set the cart upright and began to unload the crates. "Forgive me, Charlotte, I'm just not in a very good mood today."

"I imagine not. I'm very sorry for your loss. What a tragedy."

"Yes, quite a tragedy." He sniffled again. "I'm trying not to think about it. I can barely focus when I do. She was such a good woman. Such a nice person. How does this happen to someone like that?"

"I'm not sure. I've tried to understand the whys of life and loss for a long time, and the only thing I've come to realize, is that it never makes sense. At least, not to me."

"You're right about that." He sighed as he unloaded the last crate. "I'd better get going, I'm running behind schedule."

"I wasn't sure if you would be delivering today. Is the farm operating?"

"Yes. The farm workers are all there. I'm not sure for how long. Everything is up in the air right now." He looked into her eyes. "I'm sorry that I was late. I'll be on time tomorrow. And if I hear anything about the farm shutting down, I will let you know."

"Thank you." Charlotte walked him back through the door and into the shop. Many more customers had come in. He made his way through them, without sparing a smile to anyone.

"Poor soul." Charlotte touched her hand to her chest. "He's so broken up about Gladys."

"They must have been good friends." Ally

hurried over to the counter to help a waiting customer.

Charlotte watched as Isaac disappeared into the milk truck. She couldn't help but wonder if there might be more to his emotions. Did he know something about Gladys' death? Was someone keeping him silent? She vowed that she would ask him more questions when she had the chance.

CHAPTER 6

*A*fter a very busy day, Charlotte was relieved when it was time to close up. Her head spun, not from exhaustion, but from the uncertainty of all of the rumors she'd heard that day. Everyone that came in seemed to have an opinion about what happened to Gladys. None of them were kind, and she guessed that most weren't factual. But that didn't mean they didn't grab her attention. Just like the rest of the town, she wanted to know what happened, and she was certain that she wouldn't be able to rest until she did.

"Ready, Mee-Maw?" Ally walked out from the kitchen with the large box of chocolates in her hands.

"Yes, just about." Charlotte checked on a few more things in the shop, then followed Ally outside. As Ally locked the door, she watched the people on the sidewalks. Despite the fact that Valentine's Day was soon there was a lack of excitement in the air. Gladys' death weighed heavily on everyone. Once at the car she settled in the passenger side and listened as Ally flipped through the radio stations until she found something mild but peppy.

"It's a bit of a drive to get out there." She glanced at her grandmother. "Are you doing okay?"

"Yes, I'm all right, Ally, don't worry." With the box of chocolates in her lap, Charlotte gazed out through the windshield. Despite how beautiful the town was, it felt a bit eerie at twilight. There were patches of woods interspersed with homes, and the further out they drove, the more distant the houses became from one another. The streetlights also became more spread apart. She wondered what it would be like to walk along the barren road, with almost nowhere to turn to for help. Her thoughts turned to Ally in the driver's seat.

"I never really thought about how desolate it is out here."

"I think it's pretty." Ally smiled as she steered through a curve. "It's nice to get away from town, even though it's not exactly busy there. It's good to be away from the buildings and what traffic there is."

"I suppose. We haven't even passed another car since we've been driving on this road." Charlotte looked back through the windshield in time to see a pair of oncoming headlights. "I stand corrected." She laughed.

"No, I know what you mean. It seems pretty isolated. Bernice's house is up here on the right." She tilted her head towards the next curve in the road.

"I wonder how she's dealing with all of this." Charlotte patted the top of the box of chocolates. "This will never be enough to even begin to comfort that kind of wound."

"No, it won't, but I'm sure she will be grateful for it." Ally's jaw tensed as she thought of what it was like to lose her own mother. Nothing could fix it. Not chocolates, or all of the riches in the world. She parked in front of the house on the street, as she didn't want to block the driveway. There was one car in it, with a picture of a stick figure family holding hands. As they approached the front door, Ally noticed how the porch was freshly swept, and the chairs were arranged at a perfect angle.

Charlotte knocked on the door, and a second

later was greeted by loud barking from inside. A woman swiftly opened the door.

"Quiet, Bones!" She shouted at the dog. "Quiet!" Then she turned to look at the two women at her door. "Yes?"

"Hi, Bernice, I'm not sure if you remember me, but I'm Charlotte Sweet. I run the chocolate shop in town." She offered her hand to shake.

"I remember you." She smiled and shook her hand. "What brings you all the way out here?"

"My granddaughter, Ally, and I just wanted to offer you our sympathies." She gazed into the woman's eyes with a soft frown.

"It's not much." Ally held up the box of chocolates. "I'm very sorry for your loss."

"Oh, thank you so much." She grabbed the box and took a deep breath of the chocolate scent. "This is just what I needed. Do you want to come in for a moment?"

"That would be lovely, thank you." Charlotte smiled as the woman stepped out of the doorway to allow them inside. Despite the neat and tidy porch, the inside of the house was in total chaos. There were toys strewn in all directions, leftover lunch plates on the floor and the coffee table, and even a pile of dirty laundry in the middle of the living room floor. Ally gazed with a bit of shock, but Charlotte didn't seem to notice. Instead she smiled at the three children that ran up to her to greet her.

"Hi, little ones." She ruffled each of their heads. "How are you doing?"

"Play?" A little girl, not more than three, thrust her doll up towards her.

"Oh sweetie, I would love to play with you, but I'm afraid I can't stay long. What a pretty doll you have there."

"Thanks!" She giggled and then threw her doll at her older brother's head.

"Mom!" The boy, about five, shrieked. "She hit me!"

The youngest, walked towards Ally, sat down in front of her and poked at her shoe. Ally smiled down at him.

"Hi there." She waved to him.

"Sorry, they're a little wound up. Things have been a little chaotic around here today." She sighed. "And the place isn't company ready."

"Bernice." Charlotte placed a hand on her shoulder and looked into her eyes. "You have suffered a great loss. Don't stress yourself over little things. Is there any way I can help?"

"No, it's okay. I just need to stir the pot on the

stove and I'll be right back in." She headed into the kitchen which was positioned just off the living room. The smallest child followed right after her. "Please, sit down, wherever you can find a spot!" She called back from the kitchen.

Ally eyed the couch. A Great Dane was sprawled across it. He gazed at her with his big eyes as if she was nuts for thinking he would share.

"Get down now, get down, boy." Charlotte shooed him off the couch.

Ally settled down beside her. From the kitchen, Bernice shouted orders at her children. Some they listened to, some they did not, but mostly they wrestled and fought over toys.

Ally was stunned by the noise level, and the constant movement. She'd been around children of course, but not that often, and as an only child she'd never had any sibling rivalry to endure.

When Bernice returned to the living room, she had two cups of tea in her hands. Ally's heart softened as she realized that even though the woman was so busy, and grieving, she had thought to make them both something to drink.

"Thank you." Ally smiled at her as she took the cup. "You have a lovely family."

"Lovely?" She grinned. "Mya, do not ride that

dog! He is not a horse!" She rolled her eyes then looked back at Ally. "They say it gets easier. I can only hope. I want to thank you both for the candies, they will help me through this. I know that my mother was well known in the town and everyone keeps calling to check on me, but honestly, I'm okay."

Charlotte studied her eyes and noticed that there was no swelling or redness. It didn't look as if she'd been crying at all. She opened her mouth to ask her about Gladys, but before she could the front door swung open.

A tall man walked in wearing neck to toe coveralls that were stained with grease and other forms of grime.

"Daddy." Mya ran over to him and hugged his legs.

"What's this, company?" He looked from his wife, to the women on the couch. "You didn't tell me we were having anyone over."

"Oh, we didn't call ahead." Ally frowned as she realized that maybe they should have. "We just wanted to offer our condolences and drop off some chocolates."

"I see." He eyed her for a moment, then shifted his attention to Charlotte. "That's kind of you."

"It's no trouble. We've been using Bloomdale Dairy Farm as our source of milk for years, and I just want to offer my sympathies for your loss."

"Oh, thanks." He brushed off a child that had attached to his leg. "Yeah, we'll keep delivering until the sale is final."

"I haven't signed any paperwork." Bernice turned to look at him with a frown. "I know that I supported the sale before, but now that Mom is no longer here I feel like I have to honor and fight for her wishes. This is not what Mom would have wanted, and you know that."

"Maybe not, but we can't handle a dairy farm, Bernice, be reasonable, we can barely handle a kid farm." He made a funny face at the youngest child. He smiled at first, then burst into tears. "See?" He shook his head. "There's no question about it, we're selling."

"But the farm workers practically run the farm. All we need is a supervisor to keep things organized. That's it." She crossed her arms. "It's my decision."

"You listen to me, it is ridiculous to even consider keeping that farm after what Grainder has offered."

"Maybe we should go." Charlotte stood up as she detected the scent of something burning in the kitchen. She knew things were only going to get uglier.

"Yes, I'm sorry, that would probably be best." Bernice sighed as her husband continued to argue with her and the children began to plead for dinner.

By the time Ally stepped outside, she was exhausted, and she had only been watching.

"That poor woman." Ally grimaced. "How can she put up with all of that?"

"One day you'll find out." Charlotte winked at her.

"No, never." Ally laughed as she walked back to the car.

"We'll see." Charlotte grinned.

CHAPTER 7

*O*nce back in the car Charlotte and Ally drove towards the farm. It was a slow drive because there was a large tractor in the road ahead of them.

"Interesting that the two of them aren't on the same page about selling the farm." Ally stared at the tractor as it inched along. "I sensed more than just a little argument was about to happen."

"Me too. I feel a little badly for Bernice, I hope that she can handle herself against that brute." Charlotte narrowed her eyes.

"Brute?" Ally looked over at her. "Did you really think he was that bad? He was frustrated, yes, but I don't think he would do anything to harm her."

"Ally, just having a man try to force you into a decision you don't agree with is being harmed. It was her mother's farm, now it's hers, why should he get a say in what happens to it?"

"While I agree that no one should ever be forced into a decision, I have to say that his opinion on the matter should be heard. They're a family, even if she is the one who inherited the farm. That doesn't mean that he won't be affected by her decision to keep it. He might be more aware of their financial situation, and may feel it's a terrible idea." Ally sighed as she resisted leaning on the horn. It seemed to her that the tractor driver actually slowed down because she was behind him. The road was too narrow, with ditches on either side, for her to go around him.

"Well, if the rumors are true he is in a lot of financial trouble, so that may be why he is pushing for the sale of the farm as soon as possible." Charlotte tensed in her seat as she thought about the possibilities. "Of course, that could also be a motive for him to kill his mother-in-law. She wasn't going anywhere any time soon, and he needed the money right then."

"Good point." Ally frowned. "I wonder if she ever considered selling it. I'm sure they're offering a big sum."

"Probably not. The farm was probably not so

much about money to her, but more about family, history, and all of the hard work she put into it. I wouldn't be surprised if she turned down a very lucrative offer for the place. It would be like me selling the cottage. I mean I know one day it will have to be put on the market, when it's too small for you, but I'm just glad it won't be me that has to do it."

"No way. I don't ever want to sell the cottage. It's full of good memories for me."

"It is?" Charlotte looked over at her as Ally finally turned into the farm.

"Yes, of course." Ally smiled at her. "Did you think otherwise?"

"Well, I wondered, since it was such a hard time for both of us."

"Wonder no more, Mee-Maw, you were amazing to me, and I always felt so loved and welcomed in the cottage. It's still my favorite place to be."

"Good, that makes me feel better." She patted her knee.

As they parked in the long driveway that led up to the farm, Ally noticed that there were a few other cars gathered near the farmhouse. She hadn't intended to meet with anyone other than Marlo, and she wondered who the cars might belong to. They'd just left Bernice's house and as far as she knew she was the only family that Gladys had. She quickly turned off the headlights and hoped that they hadn't been spotted.

"I wonder who else is here?" Charlotte peered through the last of the evening light in the direction of the cars. "I didn't expect anyone to be here."

"Me either. I think we should be careful as we walk up. Who knows who might be out here trying to get a look at the crime scene."

"Like us?" Charlotte cast a grin in her direction.

"Not exactly. We're here for a reason. Other people are just checking things out for thrills."

"Okay, good point." Charlotte stepped out of the car as Ally stepped out of the other side. They met in front of the car and began walking up the driveway towards the parked cars. As they approached, Ally could hear voices. She looked over at her grandmother with wide eyes.

Charlotte nodded. They needed to get closer to hear better. She led the way to a few bushes that lined the walkway to the farmhouse. As they crouched down behind them, they could hear the voices more clearly.

"I did the job, and now you owe me the money," a short man said. He had a bushy black mustache, and a light blue suit jacket that did not match his black pants.

"I'll get you the money, just relax," the man across from him spoke in a soothing tone. He wore a much nicer suit. "Just give me a few days to get things straightened out."

"I don't work for air," the first man snarled. "You were supposed to pay me this morning. What's the hold up?"

"Well, things took an interesting turn, don't you think? I just need a few days. All right?"

"Fine." The short man huffed. Then he turned and stalked back to his car. The other man stared after him. Something about the way he stood, and the fierceness of his gaze, made Ally's muscles tense. He held himself as if he was important, a president, or a king, as if he shouldn't be questioned. Men like that, who believed they were powerful, could be very dangerous.

"What was that about?" Charlotte looked over at Ally. "Did that man look familiar to you?"

"Neither of them did." Ally frowned as she stared after the man who got into his car. "I don't think they're from around here at all. If they are, I've never seen them."

"Interesting." Charlotte watched as the car

drove by. She managed to snap a quick picture of the car, but missed the license plate. "Ally, try to get the license plate on that car." She pointed to the car that belonged to the man in the fine suit. He had already turned on the engine. Ally did her best to get a picture of his license plate, but it was a little blurry.

"That's the best I could do." She showed the picture to her grandmother.

"That's pretty good. Luke should be able to get enough of the numbers to run the plates." She met Ally's eyes. "Do you think he will?"

"I don't know. All I can do is ask, right?" She smiled, then sent the picture off to Luke in a text. "I'm sure when he gets a free moment he'll let me know one way or the other." She turned her attention back to the farm.

"It's pretty clear that they had some kind of deal going. I hate to think it, but what if it has to do with Gladys' death?" Charlotte turned to look at Ally.

"It's possible, well, probable really. But, why would they be so bold as to meet out here on the farm? That seems pretty risky to me." She sighed. "I keep thinking about Parker being a mechanic. He would easily know how to cut the brake lines, and that it would result in a crash."

"That's true, but I think that's also pretty common knowledge. I can see that he would have motive to inherit the farm, to solve his financial trouble, but this is his wife's mother we're talking about. I don't know, he'd have to be pretty heartless to do it."

"People can be pretty heartless." Ally stood up behind the bushes and stared out over the farm. The farm was quiet and still. In the distance she knew that the cows were lined up in barns and probably not silent, but their sounds didn't reach the house. To her, in that moment, the farm looked like a ghost town, abandoned by its occupants. Gladys had loved the property as if it were the love of her life, and Ally guessed she would try to hang on to it. The soil, the buildings, even the sky, was full of Gladys' presence. She closed her eyes and just listened. She imagined she could hear Gladys' voice on the light breeze. Not her voice, but a soft whistling. Her body jolted as she realized the whistling wasn't in her imagination, but truly carried on the breeze, and headed in their direction.

Charlotte heard the noise as well. Without the headlights on it was hard to make out anything at a distance.

"What is that, Ally?" She looked over at her

granddaughter, whose eyes were wide. "Do you hear it, too?"

"Yes, I do," Ally whispered back. "I can't tell where it's coming from." She squinted into the darkness. Then suddenly she saw a flash of light, followed by others. It was eerie at first, because of the way it swung back and forth. Then she realized it was a flashlight.

"Look, there are the farm workers heading back to the barn. It must have been one of them whistling. I want to see if I can spot Marlo." She walked boldly out from behind the bushes and headed in the direction of the farm workers.

The group of mostly men gathered together close to the barn. She watched as a man who appeared to be in charge began handing out what she assumed were daily wages. She was certain that Marlo would be there. If he was paid each day, then he wouldn't want to miss his payment for the day. As she scanned through the faces she searched for his familiar face. Finally, towards the back she spotted him. She stepped forward as the crowd began to disperse.

"Marlo?" She called out to him as he started to turn away. "Marlo, wait!" She took a few fast steps towards him. "Please, I just want to talk to you. That's all."

He reluctantly turned to face her. She could tell from the tightness of his shoulders that he did not really want to be standing there in front of her. However, she was relieved that he was willing to speak to her.

"Yes, what is it?" He shoved his hands in his pockets.

"Last night, you wanted to tell me something, didn't you?" She held his gaze.

"No, nothing." He lowered his eyes. "Nothing at all."

"Marlo, you don't have to keep the truth from me. I'm not going to cause you any trouble. I just want you to know, if you have something you want to say, I'm willing to listen."

"I can't." He closed his eyes tight, then opened them slowly. "I never should have come there. I'm sorry about that. I didn't mean to scare you."

"It's all right, Marlo, I'm not afraid." She took another step towards him. "If there's anything you know that you think might help solve Gladys' murder, you have to tell me."

"It was awful." He rubbed his hand along the back of his neck. "It wasn't my fault."

Those words made Ally shiver on the inside. She heard her grandmother approaching from behind her, but she waved her back. She didn't want the presence of another person to spook Marlo out of speaking. Why would he think he had to insist it wasn't his fault? Was it possible that he didn't just know something about the murder, but was involved in it as well? The thought was more than a little disturbing to her as she stood so close to him.

"I'm sure it wasn't you, Marlo. Someone cut the brake lines on that quad bike, though. Someone had to have access to it. Who do you think might do that?"

"No." He shook his head. "I don't know. I didn't see anything." He sighed and looked back at her again. "It wasn't my fault."

"Who said that it was?" She took another step towards him, so that she could speak in a hushed tone. "Did someone tell you that it was your fault?"

"No!" His eyes grew wide. "It wasn't my fault! No! No!" He shook his head from side to side, shaking it again and again. Ally was startled by the motions. Charlotte stepped up beside her and drew her back a few steps.

"He's having a moment," she murmured. "He's worked up."

One of the other workers jogged over to them.

"Marlo, what is it?" The taller man frowned. "What's wrong? What did you do to him?" The man turned his attention on them.

"Nothing." Ally still stared at Marlo as he continued to shake his head and kept shouting no over and over again. "I was just talking with him. Is he okay?"

"He has some problems." The man patted his shoulder. "Marlo, it's all right. Calm down now. Do your breathing."

Marlo took a deep breath, then another. He stopped shaking his head. He stared hard at Ally, then he turned and walked away. Ally stared after him, confused.

"Does he often do that?" She looked at the man before her.

"Only when he's upset. I haven't seen him do it in a while. Whatever you were talking to him about must have really bothered him." He eyed them. "What are you doing out here?"

"Nothing." Charlotte grabbed Ally's hand and pulled her away from the man. "We need to get out of here, Ally. Something doesn't feel right."

Ally nodded. She was still rattled by Marlo's wild actions. One moment he seemed perfectly lucid and able to communicate, the next it was like he no longer even saw her. She'd never witnessed anything like it before.

"I didn't mean to upset him." Ally swallowed back a rush of guilt as she got back into the car.

"It's all right. It wasn't your fault. You couldn't have known." Charlotte buckled her seat belt.

Those words played through Ally's mind. It wasn't your fault. Marlo kept repeating the same statement, it wasn't his fault. But there had to be a reason he thought he needed to make that clear.

"He was so agitated. I wonder what set him off?" Ally rubbed her hands along the steering wheel and tried to focus on what Marlo had said to her.

"Clearly he's upset about Gladys' death." Charlotte glanced over at her. "Maybe he had something to do with it."

"Maybe." Ally continued to squeeze the steering wheel without turning on the car. "But it seemed more like he was scared. Like, he thought he was going to be in trouble for something that he didn't do."

"Or that he was going to be in trouble for something he did do." Charlotte shook her head. "Maybe Gladys did something to set him off, and he reacted by killing her. It's possible. We should find out what we can about him and how he was connected to Gladys on a personal level. Did he act like that at all when you first met him?"

"No, not at all. He seemed nervous, and shy, but nothing like that." Ally sighed. "I'm sure he knows something about Gladys' murder. But how can we find out what it is if I can't talk to him without upsetting him?" ·

"Maybe Luke will have better luck. I'm sure he will be checking out everyone that works on the farm."

"You're right." Ally turned the engine on. As they drove away from the farm the memory of Marlo's wide eyes haunted her. What had him so frightened? Was it the thought of being caught for what he did or the thought of someone else finding out what he knew?

CHAPTER 8

*A*lly dropped her grandmother off at Freely Lakes, then headed back to the cottage. Her mind was filled with a multitude of questions and very few answers. Just when she thought she had a pretty good handle on who might be responsible for Gladys' death, a new question popped up. A question about Marlo, and the mystery men who had met at the farm, and of course, Parker who had the strongest motive of all.

When Ally arrived at the cottage she was greeted with the usual chaos of hungry animals. She fed them, while sharing a bit about her day, then put a quick dinner together for herself. When she sat down on the couch, she felt her exhaustion for the first time. It had been a very busy day made longer by the visit to Bernice's house, and Bloomdale farm.

She realized that she would need to get up to manage a very busy shop in the morning. She guessed the shop might be even busier as they were getting closer to Valentine's Day. She'd just finished her food, when her phone rang. When she saw Luke's name on the screen she picked it up quickly.

"Hi sweetie, how are you doing?"

"I've got a little information on that picture you sent me." Luke's voice was strained, and quiet, as if he was trying not to be heard.

"Great. Are you okay?" She frowned.

"Sorry, I'm hiding from an over-eager police officer that has a million questions for me." He sighed. "It's good to have fresh blood, but wow this rookie is determined to talk my ear off."

"Poor guy." Ally smiled. Luke wasn't the overly talkative type. He liked a good chat, but then preferred to have a break. "I went out to the farm last night and spoke to Marlo, one of the workers there." She shared with him her experience at the shop, and then at the farm. "I can't help feeling like he knows something about the murder. Or maybe he even had a part in it. Have you spoken to him?"

"We're working our way through the farm work-ers, but I'll definitely move him up to the top of the list. I don't like that he came to the shop. That worries me. If you see him hanging out there again, you need to let me know, got it?"

"Got it. But I don't think he wants to hurt me. It was more like he wanted to speak to you about something, but then was too scared to go through with it."

"All right, I'll check it out. Now, it's my turn for questions. Where did you see the car that you took a picture of?"

"At the farm tonight. There were two cars, but the picture of the other one came out too blurry to be useful."

"Send that to me, too. I might be able to get it to be clearer."

"Sure I will, but why? What did you find?"

"Well, the owner of the car is Rick, the representative from Grainder that was trying to finalize the sale of Bloomdale. I'm very curious about who he was meeting with, but there are no cameras on the property."

"Wow, he struck me as someone who thought he was important." She frowned.

"You talked with him?"

"No, I just listened while he spoke with the other man. They were arguing about money. One said he did the job and wanted to get paid, and Rick said that he just had to wait, he would have the money soon. I guess maybe he's waiting for the sale to go through?" Her stomach churned. "Oh, Luke do you think that other man could have been an assassin?"

"It's possible. We won't know anything until we figure out who he is. Could you describe him to me?"

"Shortish, and small. Honestly, I didn't get a good look at him, he had a hat on, and it was just about dark."

"Okay, well any pictures you have of his car just send them to me and I'll see if I can get a tech here to enhance it."

"Good, I'll send it to you right now. Sorry I didn't get more. Now I wish I'd gotten a better picture of the shorter man."

"Ally, I know you're going to do what you're going to do, and I trust your instincts, but you need to keep in mind that this could be a very dangerous man. Actually, any of these people could be very dangerous. I know it is pointless to tell you to stay out of this, but I wish you would. You have to make sure that you are being careful."

"I am, always."

"Just promise me you'll be careful."

"I will, Luke. Promise me that you're going to get some sleep."

"I'll try. Love you."

"Love you, too." She hung up the phone and sent the blurry picture to him, then placed a call to her grandmother to update her on the situation.

"So, the man we saw was Rick?"

"Yes, and he works for Grainder."

"Maybe he hired the other man to kill Gladys?" Charlotte's voice wavered as she spoke.

"Maybe. I don't know, Mee-Maw, something isn't fitting together for me. Maybe I need a little sleep."

"I know I do." Charlotte yawned into the phone. "We'll talk about it in the morning, hmm? Are you going to pick me up?"

"Yes, I'll be there. Good night, Mee-Maw, I hope you're able to sleep tonight."

"Me too."

Ally hung up the phone, then stretched out on the couch. Soon, Peaches was perched on her stomach. Her solid purr sent vibrations through all of her muscles, which helped her to relax. She closed her eyes and took a deep breath. Peaches protested with a soft meow as she stretched her body into the air, then sunk back down again.

"Sorry Peaches." She stroked her head. "I'm just trying to find some peace."

Peaches bumped her chin with her head, then rubbed her cheek along hers. Ally smiled.

"Thanks. That helps a lot." She snuggled into the couch and let her mind drift on the sound of the cat's subtle snores.

~

Charlotte woke the next morning from a deep sleep. She hadn't dreamed, that she could recall, but she felt as if she'd slept enough to make up for a week's worth of insomnia. She wasn't sure why she'd been able to sleep so well, but it might have had something to do with the man snoring on her couch. She crept past him as she headed to the bathroom. He'd shown up the night before and offered to stay to keep her company. Something about his presence made her comfortable enough to fall asleep. But now she had to hurry to get ready as Ally would be there to pick her up any minute.

As Charlotte moved through the apartment, careful not to wake him, a subtle warmth brewed within her. It was nice having someone else in her home. For so long she had lived with Ally, then she went off to live her own life, and when she returned they'd shared the cottage for some time.

She did love her independence, and having her own space to enjoy, but there was something very comforting about the presence of another. She left a short note for him, then grabbed a bagel before she headed to the door. Just as she reached it there was a light knock from the other side. She opened the door and smiled at Ally.

"Good morning."

"Good morning." She held up a cup of coffee and a bagel.

"I'll take the coffee, but I already have a bagel." She stepped out through the door in a bit of a rush. She didn't want to have to answer questions about why Jeff was on her couch. As she locked the door behind her Ally gave her a light pat on the shoulder.

"Did you sleep well?"

"Yes, thankfully. What about you?"

"Not so great." Ally frowned. "But enough. I just hope Luke made some headway on finding Rick."

"Me too. Maybe all of this will be wrapped up by the end of the day, or at least before Valentine's Day."

"Speaking of which, did you find out what Jeff is planning for your special date?"

"Special date." Charlotte rolled her eyes as they reached the parking lot. "It's no big deal, just a night to spend together. At this point, I'm not sure that we'll be able to go through with it. I can't see me enjoying whatever he has in store, while distracted by Gladys' unsolved murder."

"Hopefully it won't be unsolved for much longer." Ally opened the door to her car, then looked across the top at her grandmother. "No, not hopefully, I'm going to make sure of it."

"We're going to make sure of it." Charlotte climbed into the car beside her. "But first we need to get the shop open. I'm sure we will be twice as busy as yesterday."

When they pulled up to the shop, they were both greeted with a surprise.

"Oh dear, Mee-Maw, look." Ally pointed towards the shop. There was a line of five people standing outside the locked door. "It looks like people are starting to remember that Valentine's Day is only a few days away."

"Yes, it does." Charlotte waved to the people waiting as they pulled into the parking lot, then glanced at her. "Are you ready for this?"

"I think so." Ally grinned. "It'll be good to get our mind off things for a little while. Let's see how many chocolates we can make today. If we have a nice surplus we can even sell some online."

"All right, your enthusiasm is hard to ignore." Charlotte smiled. "Let's do this!"

As they unlocked the front door they chatted with the people who waited. They wanted to get their purchases done before they headed off to work for the day. It didn't take long to ring them up and send them on their way. Once that first rush subsided, Ally headed into the back to work on making more chocolates, while Charlotte completed the tasks they had skipped in order to take care of the customers. She was lost in the monotony of running the broom across the floor, when she heard the door swing open. She looked up with a smile at the woman who stepped in. She looked to be a few years younger than Charlotte, with blonde hair cut into a short bob and speckled with gray streaks. She had a round physique, and though she walked with a slight hitch in her step, she presented herself with a good amount of confidence. Charlotte noticed right away that she didn't smile back.

"Hello there. How are you today?" Charlotte set

the broom against the wall and walked back over to the counter.

"Not good." She huffed as she strode towards the counter.

"I'm sorry to hear that. Is there a chocolate in particular I can interest you in?" Charlotte studied the woman's face. It wasn't just that she didn't smile. She seemed upset. She couldn't help but wonder what might be bothering her. The woman didn't even look at the chocolates on display. Instead she reached into her inside jacket pocket and pulled something out. It looked like just a slip of paper at first, then she noticed that it was a photograph.

"I'm just here for some information." She thrust the photograph down on the counter between them.

"Okay." Charlotte looked away from the woman, down at the picture, and instantly recognized the man in it. "That's Isaac." She looked back up at her. "What kind of information do you want about him?"

"He's my husband." Her cheeks grew pink as she continued. "I want to know if he came here."

"Yes, he was in here." Charlotte looked into her eyes. "He delivers our milk, from Bloomdale farm. Are you looking for him?"

"He bought candy here, didn't he?" She looked between both of them with a sharp gaze.

"Yes, he did." She frowned. "Was there something wrong with it? We can replace the box if something was wrong." Charlotte stepped closer to her. "You seem so upset."

"I am upset." She narrowed her eyes. "How many boxes of candy did he buy from you?"

Charlotte's eyes widened as she realized the path of the conversation. The tension in the shop grew thick. It seemed coincidental that despite how busy they had been, in that moment there wasn't another soul to help, and no one who stepped in the door to interrupt. Charlotte stalled as she tried to think of the best way to answer the woman. Yes, Isaac had bought two boxes of candy, but that was his personal business, wasn't it? She had no right to share that information with his wife, who clearly suspected that he had purchased multiple boxes of candy. She could easily assume from the anger in the woman's expression that this was not about her husband overspending or holding out on candy. She believed that he had bought candy for someone other than her, and she intended to find the proof by getting a response from Charlotte. Her heart slammed against her chest as she tried to decide what she should do. A quick glance at Ally showed some confusion in her own expression.

"Please, just tell me the truth." The woman stared hard at Charlotte. "Just tell me how many boxes he bought."

Charlotte swallowed hard as she knew that her response might change the woman's marriage forever.

Ally looked over at her grandmother. For some reason it seemed as if she couldn't speak. She wasn't sure why she was hesitating to answer the woman. She was certain they both knew how many boxes of candy Isaac bought.

"I'm not sure I recall." Charlotte finally responded, then glanced over at Ally.

"Ma'am, what's wrong? What can we help you with?" Ally took a step forward. She was a bit stunned that her grandmother would avoid the truth, but was sure she had a good reason for it.

"I told you exactly how you can help me. I want to know how many boxes of candy my husband bought. Are you going to tell me or not?" She glared at both of them.

"I can't recall either, sorry." Ally locked her eyes to the other woman's. "We are very busy at the moment, because it's Valentine's Day soon so it's difficult keeping track."

"I bet he bought two." She laughed, as tears

sprang to her eyes. "One for me and I think the other one for his girlfriend." She glanced over at Charlotte. "There's no reason to protect him."

"It isn't my intention to protect him, I just don't want to be involved in something that is not my business. It's easy to jump to conclusions, and much harder to take the time to find out the truth. Perhaps you're just interpreting things wrong." She touched the woman's shoulder. "Your husband seems like a very nice person."

"Yes, he seems that way doesn't he." She snorted. "He seems that way to everyone. He's even very nice to me. Always courteous, always considerate. He bought me my favorite candies. And I'm sure he bought her favorite candies as well. Every day I wake up and I tell myself, Harriet, this is it, this is the day you put an end to all of this and start a new life. Then he looks into my eyes, he kisses my cheek, and I hope that maybe, just maybe, he's become the husband he promised to be."

"Harriet, I'm sorry you're dealing with this." Ally frowned as she looked between her and her grandmother. "But finding out how many boxes of candy he bought won't fix anything. You need to communicate with him, find out the whole story, and then start making your choices."

"I know, I know." She sighed and wiped at her eyes. "I didn't mean to come in here and cause you any trouble. I just wanted to know, for sure."

"Well, unfortunately I can't recall. Do you want some hot chocolate, or some coffee?" Charlotte took her hand in hers. "You can sit, and chat a bit. It might help."

"No, I'm sorry. I need to go. I need to talk to him and find out the whole truth. There's just no point in pretending anymore." She started to turn towards the door.

"Are you sure you're going to be okay?" Charlotte walked beside her. "If there's anything we can do—"

"I'll be okay." She turned and offered a sad smile to each of them. "Even though you didn't answer me, I have the answers I needed." She slammed her hand against the door and strode out with rigid, furious steps. Ally was a little startled by the way she carried herself.

Charlotte stared after her, her lips pursed and her eyes wide.

CHAPTER 9

*A*fter Harriet had left the shop Charlotte and Ally began tidying up the display counters.

"Do you really think that Isaac is cheating on her? He seems like such a nice person." Ally placed a platter in the refrigerator.

"I can't say." Charlotte shook her head. "But I think he's about to have a very difficult day."

"Why didn't you tell her about the two boxes of chocolates, Mee-Maw?" She glanced over at her.

"I just don't think it's my place. Living in this town, I've learned it's best to try to stay out of everyone's business." She looked at her grand-daughter. "She already knew the truth, she didn't need us to confirm it. I just hope they're able to get it worked out."

The door swung open, and Mrs. Bing rushed through it, her eyes wide.

"Was that Harriet that just left here?"

"Yes, do you know her?" Ally cringed as she realized what a foolish question that was. Mrs. Bing knew pretty much everyone in Blue River and the surrounding towns.

"That's Isaac's wife. She looked upset." Mrs. Bing glanced over her shoulder. "Did she finally find out?"

"Find out what?" Charlotte eyed her with a raised eyebrow.

"Well, that Isaac is cheating on her of course." She spoke in a hushed voice, but there was so much excitement in her whisper it was difficult to subdue.

"Mrs. Bing, are you sure about that, or is it just a rumor?" Ally studied her expression intently.

"Well, it's not as if I've seen him do it myself. But it's pretty well known." She frowned. "At least to everyone but her. I guess that's changed now." She glanced over her shoulder to be sure that no one else was in the shop, then looked back at Ally. "Recently, I've seen her following him around. She will drive behind his milk truck on his route sometimes. I've seen them argue about it. He is always very calm

with her, but she will holler and wave her arms."
She squinted her eyes. "She causes quite a scene."

"Wow, she must really suspect him." Would she
be so angry that she would cause some kind of harm
to Isaac? She hoped that wouldn't be the case, but
she couldn't be sure. "All I know is that she was
quite upset." Ally sighed and shook her head. "It
seems to me that Valentine's Day is not working any
magic this year."

"Maybe not." Mrs. Bing popped a chocolate into
her mouth. "But it still tastes delicious."

The rest of the day went by in a blur. Ally
couldn't dwell on whether she'd made the right
choice not to tell Harriet about the two boxes of
chocolates, she could barely think straight about
which chocolates to put into which boxes. Not only
were they getting orders in the shop, but also on the
phone. As she tried to navigate through all of it, she
was relieved to have her grandmother there at her
side. Without her she was sure that she would be
making all kinds of mistakes. She might have even
locked the doors to prevent more customers from
coming in. But Charlotte handled it all brilliantly.
When the line was long she joked with the
customers, and entertained them with stories about

the history of Blue River, and Valentine's Days gone by. Never once did she lose her bright smile. In the midst of it all, Ally gazed at her.

"How do you do it, Mee-Maw, how do you keep so calm in all of this chaos?"

"It's not chaos, sweetheart. It's excitement. People don't mind waiting, if they think they are waiting for something great. People don't just come in here to buy chocolates, or gifts, they come in here to have the Valentine's Day experience. So, it's important to provide that experience. Barking at them, or looking exhausted, or put off by yet another order, doesn't give them that experience. The key is to treat your customer with kindness, and gratitude, because their purchase is supporting your shop, and that makes it quite valuable."

"I'm not sure I'll ever be able to balance things the way you do." Ally's cheeks were flushed and her back was coated in sweat.

"Honey, it takes time, and it takes experience. It's not something you can just snap your fingers and become. Trust me, I paid my dues with meltdowns, there were even times I thought about shutting down the shop for good." She got pulled away by another customer. As Ally rushed to fill up a box of chocolates she thought about her grandmother's words. She'd never imagined her grandmother thinking about closing the shop. She couldn't picture what her life would be like without it. A new sense of gratitude to her grandmother washed over her. She'd fought such difficult battles, and yet there she was with a bright smile and a laugh for the customer who wanted five boxes of custom chocolates, as soon as possible. No matter how long she worked in the shop, she knew she would always have a lot to learn from her.

$\sim$

*A*t closing time, Ally and Charlotte were both worn out.

"Mee-Maw, go on home, I'll finish closing up." Ally gave her a quick kiss on the cheek.

"Are you sure? There's still a lot to do." Charlotte stifled a yawn.

"I'm absolutely sure. Go on. I want to know you're getting some rest." Ally wagged her finger at her and paired the gesture with a stern look.

"Don't start babying me now." Charlotte rolled her eyes. "I want to know that you're tucked into bed too, young lady."

"Don't worry about that, Peaches will make sure

of it." She gave her grandmother a warm hug. "Try to have a good night."

"Thanks, I will. You, too." She kissed her cheek, then headed out the door.

Once Ally was alone in the shop she began to clean up and shut everything down for the night. They'd done a great deal of business and had quite a few new customers. She could feel all of the hard work in her muscles, and the exhaustion that echoed through her. But she didn't want to head straight home, instead she had other plans.

$\sim$

*A*fter Ally left the shop she drove towards the police station. She wanted to find out a little information and Luke hadn't responded to her text yet. When she arrived she discovered that Luke was not there. That didn't surprise her as she knew that he was chasing down every lead that he could find. She was just about to leave when Errol, a friend of Luke's, and a young police officer, waved to her from the hallway.

"Hey Ally, what are you doing here?"

"I was looking for Luke." She managed a half-smile. "I just had a few questions for him."

"Well, what are they?" He shrugged. "Maybe I can help?"

"Oh, that would be great!" She followed him over to an empty desk. "Do you have access to the database?"

"Sure." He cleared his throat. "They even let me have handcuffs."

"Right, sorry." She blushed and laughed at the same time. "I'm wondering if Gladys Bloomdale filed any complaint against anyone in the past. Would you check on that for me?"

"I thought Luke was the detective?" He eyed her for a second.

"He is, I'm just curious." She did her best to hide the impatience in her voice. She wasn't sure how to explain that she was looking into the murder, she was sure if she did he would provide her with no information.

"No worries." He flashed a grin. "I've heard quite a bit about you from Luke." He turned back to the computer and began to type.

She tried not to wonder what that statement meant. How much had Luke shared and why? She didn't have time to think about it, as he tapped the screen a second later.

"It looks like she filed a complaint once before."

"Just once in all these years?" She raised an eyebrow.

"Yes, I guess she didn't have much need for police assistance. Let's see." He scrolled through the file. "Okay, actually this was earlier this month. She complained about someone following her around. She insisted that someone had been stalking her." He narrowed his eyes. "That's strange, it was dismissed the next morning, let's see why." He scrolled a bit more then nodded. "Okay, it was dismissed because her son-in-law came in to speak to the police. It appears that he showed some medical evidence that Gladys was being evaluated for some memory disorders. He explained that she'd even been found wandering the farm in a confused state. The case was closed."

"As the result of Parker's word?" She raised an eyebrow. "No one thought to question why he might want to make her look mentally incapacitated?"

"Hey, take it easy there, I didn't take the report and obviously neither did Luke. Though I'm not sure if this has come up in the investigation. I'm going to flag it and send it to Luke so that he can make sure that he reviews it. Anything else I can look up for you?"

"No, that's plenty. Thanks, Errol." She gave him a brief smile then stood up from the desk. After years of not making a single report, she'd felt concerned enough to report a possible stalker. Unfortunately, the police had believed Parker over her. Which put Parker right back at the top of the suspect list. Did he really believe his mother-in-law was imagining it, or was it a way to cover up for himself?

As Ally left the police station she couldn't help picturing what Gladys' life must have been like in the last few months. Did she feel as if everyone was turning against her? She'd fought her entire life for that farm, and as a woman she struggled to be taken seriously in an environment that was dominated by men, yet the first moment he could her son-in-law was helping someone take it all from her. Sure, she would have stood to profit from the sale as well, but not if he managed to get her declared incompetent. If he did, all of that money would be going right into his pocket. She decided that she needed to find out a bit more about him. Though it was nearing eight o'clock, she hoped the garage would still be open. When she parked in front of it there were several other cars present, and lights on inside the garage.

She approached the only door she could find and pulled it open. Inside, a circle of three men, each with a cigar in their mouth, were gathered around a small table. Cards were strewn across it along with a few crumpled up dollar bills. She realized she'd interrupted a poker game.

"We're closed for tonight, don't open again until seven tomorrow." A man with bushy hair, bushy eyebrows, and a long beard looked up at her. He seemed to be in his fifties or sixties, but it was hard to tell with all of the facial hair. The two other men at the table were quite a bit younger, but neither of them was Parker.

"I'm looking for Parker."

"Yeah? What do you want with him?" One of the other men looked up at her with a wry smile. His face was smudged with grease, but that did nothing to make him look any older. She wondered if he was even out of his teens.

"I just need to speak with him." She eyed the third man who seemed to be about Parker's age, if not a little younger. His hair was hidden by a tight ball cap, and his face was spotless, clean of any hair or grease. She guessed that he did more work behind the counter than under the cars.

"He's gone for the night. You can find him at

home I guess." He tossed a card down on the table. "One."

"Just a minute now." The older man huffed. "We can't play with this distraction."

"Listen, I'm just wondering if he's been acting any differently lately. Strange at all?" She looked between all three men.

"You a cop?" the youngest asked and bit down hard on his cigar.

"Are you old enough to smoke?" She raised an eyebrow as she stared back at him.

The oldest man burst into laughter and slapped the table.

"Yeah, you're definitely Charlotte's kin. Ain't she, Bob?" He looked over at the third man.

"Yes, that's for sure." Bob chuckled as well.

Ally's cheeks flushed. Of course, they knew her grandmother. She knew just about everyone in Blue River and the surrounding towns.

"I remember when you used to toddle around that chocolate shop." The oldest man shook his head as his laughter faded. "I guess you're grown now. But let me explain something to you, little lady, you don't need to be asking questions about people, that only gets you into trouble."

"I want to ask some questions." She placed her

hands on her hips as she studied the three men. "I suppose you would want to know if Parker was involved in something illegal and this garage was at risk of shutting down, wouldn't you?"

"At risk?" The youngest man pulled the cigar from his mouth and stared at her. "We're closing in three days. Can't get much more risky than that, now can it?"

"Oh." She blinked. "I didn't know that."

"Guess you didn't ask enough questions." The oldest man stubbed his cigar into an ashtray. "Now, if you don't mind we're trying to enjoy a game here."

"Sure." She stepped back out of the garage. A mixture of anger and embarrassment flooded through her. Clearly Parker had every intention of selling the farm, shutting down the garage, and living a life of luxury off the profit from the farm. He had an undeniable motive to get rid of his mother-in-law, and he seemed so very confident that the sale would go through, even before Gladys' death. Was that because he knew that his problem would soon be eliminated? Or had he done it himself?

As Ally started towards her car she noticed a quad bike parked near one of the closed garage doors. Surely it wasn't the same one that Gladys died on. She was sure that would have been kept by the police as evidence. But the sight of it reminded her that Parker had access to the quad bikes, and the knowledge to cut the brake lines. It was impossible not to think of him as a suspect.

CHAPTER 10

*C*harlotte walked down the hall towards her apartment. She couldn't help but think about Harriet and how upset she'd been. She wondered if the woman would be able to control herself, or if she would go home and cause some chaos with her husband. As she approached the door, she smiled at the sight of Jeff standing in front of it.

"Jeff, you're a welcome sight." Her smile widened as she paused in front of him. He held out a single, long stem rose.

"A little beauty, for my beauty." He smiled as he kissed her cheek.

"Jeff, it's lovely." She took the rose from him as her cheeks warmed with blush. "But not necessary."

"It's very necessary. I plan to make sure that you

CINDY BELL

know how much I care, every single time I see you."
He looked into her eyes. "You're just going to have
to get used to it."

"Jeff, that's sweet, but I know how much you
care." She patted his chest as she gazed into his
eyes. "You don't have to do anything special to
show me."

"How about dinner?" He smiled as he offered
his arm. "Some place nice?"

"Or maybe dinner in?" She cringed. "I'd love to
spend some time with you, but honestly I'm
exhausted. I'm in no mood to go out for dinner."

"All right, deal, as long as you let me cook. I'm
sure I can whip something up from whatever you
have in the kitchen. You have to sit, with your feet
up, and relax. Agreed?"

"Agreed." She laughed as she unlocked the
door. The thought of being waited on was a
little worrying, but she knew that his intentions
were good, and the idea of relaxing and getting
a home cooked meal was too good to turn
down. As he got to work in the kitchen, she
settled on the couch. With the open floor plan
she could easily talk with him while he was in
the kitchen. She began to update him on all of
the things they'd learned about Gladys' death,

and also about her encounter with Harriet in the shop.

"It was really disturbing to see how upset she was." She sighed.

He glanced over at her as he stirred a pot of spaghetti sauce on the stove. "What made you hide the truth from her?"

"Well, I just didn't think it was my business to share that kind of information. It's not as if she or Isaac are personal friends. Even if they were I doubt I would tell her." She stood up and joined him in the kitchen, both to be close to him, and to breathe the scent of the sauce he'd added spices to.

"So, you erred on the side of protecting him?" He turned off the pasta he'd been boiling, then carried the pot to the sink to drain it.

"Careful." She frowned as he poured the hot water off the pasta. "I don't think I was protecting him. I think I just knew that the information might be misinterpreted, and if it was, I'd be responsible for sharing it with her."

"And if she was right, and he was cheating?" He set the pot back down on the stove and added the sauce to it. "How would you feel if you knew you were protecting a cheater?"

"Again, I wasn't protecting him." She stepped up

117

beside him and met his eyes. "Why do you keep saying that I was?"

"I'm sorry, my view of the situation is probably colored by my own experiences." He grabbed two bowls out of the cabinet and began to fill them with the pasta.

"Own experiences of what? I'm confused?" She gathered some silverware and napkins to set the table with.

"With cheating." He carried the bowls over to the table. "It happened to me once, and I swore it would never happen to me again. I was hesitant for a long time to get involved with another woman, it really had a strong impact on me."

"I'm sorry, Jeff." She rubbed her hands along his shoulders before joining him at the table. "Why didn't you ever tell me about it?"

"It's a little embarrassing. It's funny, the person who cheats is the one that's done something wrong, but the person who is hurt, is the one who feels ashamed." He picked up his fork. "It was a long time ago."

"It doesn't matter how long ago it was. If it hurt you, it can last a lifetime." She frowned. "I'm sorry I was talking so casually about it, that must have been upsetting for you."

"It's not, exactly." He looked across the table at her, then took her hand. "It's just that, people can't understand it, unless they've experienced it. It seems pretty normal to me that she would be so upset."

"And it bothers you that it seems like I protected Isaac?" She ran her thumb across his knuckles and sighed. "I'm sorry. I don't condone cheating, of course I don't. But it's not my place to discuss a customer's business."

"I wouldn't think that you would. I'm sorry if I came on a little strong about it. I guess my point is that not knowing, being lied to, it's so very hurtful. And, if I had been in your position, I would have told her the truth, whether it was my business or not." He took a bite of his food. "But that's me, and it's not my place to tell you what to do."

"Do you think less of me because I didn't?"

"No, not at all." He frowned. "Please, don't take me the wrong way. You made the choice that most people make. I'm just giving you my perspective of why Harriet would have been so upset."

"Upset enough to kill?" She raised an eyebrow as she studied him.

"Are you asking me if I would have killed someone?" He stared back at her, his own expression growing more serious.

CINDY BELL

"I was asking if you thought she could be angry enough to kill." She picked up her own fork and pushed around her pasta.

"It's hard to say. But at the time I did think I would never share my heart with anyone again. The pain, the betrayal, can be extreme. If she had some mental illness to begin with, I suppose it would be possible."

"I didn't ask if you would." She met his eyes.

"I know you didn't." He smiled as he took another bite of food. "But I thought you should know. As for Harriet, are you worried about Isaac?"

"I'm not sure exactly. I just noticed something about her seemed off. Like it was more than just anger, something just a little darker." She shook her head. "I don't know, it's possible that I was just too caught up in all of this, and I'm seeing things that aren't there."

"Oh no, I don't think that's possible. You're one of the sharpest people I know." He pointed to the pasta. "Eat, you need your strength. Honestly, I'd be more concerned about the person he was having the affair with. Do you know who he bought the other box of chocolates for?"

"Not a clue." She shrugged and took a bite of her food. "Mm, so good. Honestly, I didn't even

120

think much about it. Lots of people buy more than one box. They buy some for their girlfriend, their mother, their co-workers, it's not uncommon."

"It's also not uncommon for someone to have a wandering eye, or heart. Do you believe her?"

"Yes, I do." She stared down at her food. "I wish I didn't, because I like Isaac, he seems like a very nice man. But I don't think a woman would be that outraged if she didn't have some solid evidence that something is going on."

"You may be right about that. But jealousy can be a very ugly thing." He sighed, then took another bite of his food. "Not a very romantic conversation is it?"

"No." She smiled as she gazed across the table at him. "But it is the best company."

"Thanks." Jeff smiled at her in return and met her eyes. "I enjoy any time I spend with you, Charlotte. I'm looking forward to Valentine's Day."

"Me too." She swallowed down her pasta with a slight cough. As much as she wanted her statement to be true, it wasn't quite. She was looking forward to spending time with him, but with how focused he was on it, she was worried that he might want more from her than she was ready for and the last thing she wanted to do was hurt his feelings.

"Are you okay?" He pushed her glass towards her, his eyes filled with concern.

She took a sip of her water, then nodded.

"Yes, I'm fine. Just too big of a bite." She gazed into his eyes again. She hoped that he was happy to keep things the way they were, at least for a while.

CHAPTER 11

*A*lly arrived early to open up the shop. She was determined to get ahead on the chocolates so they would be able to do a bit more investigating. As she began to go through the process of opening up she realized they were getting very low on milk again. A glance at the clock told her that the delivery, if there was going to be one, should be arriving soon. Her muscles tensed at the thought of seeing Isaac. Would he know that his wife had come in asking questions about the chocolates he purchased? Would he suspect they told her something to incriminate him? She suddenly realized just why her grandmother stayed out of things. Doing the opposite could lead to very difficult situations. When her cell phone buzzed it startled her. She grabbed it from her pocket and saw that Luke was calling.

"Hello?" She smiled as she heard his voice.

"Hi there. How are you this morning?"

"Good, and dying to talk to you." Before he could say another word she launched into her experience at the garage the night before. "I'm telling you, Luke, I really think that Parker is behind all of this. I mean he stood to gain so much from her death."

"Just a moment, Ally." He cleared his throat. "I see what you see, too. But Parker has an alibi. He was at the meeting with Rick, waiting for Gladys to arrive. Before that he was at home with Bernice. There are no holes that I can find in his alibi."

"Well, maybe he cut the brake lines the night before." Ally frowned.

"Then the quad bike would have crashed much earlier. It was driven out to the fields before Gladys returned. Someone had to cut those lines between the time it was taken out to the field and the time she drove it back. I agree, Parker is the best suspect, but unfortunately at this time, he is also the only suspect I have that has an alibi. With Rick there with him at the meeting he has a pretty good alibi, too."

"That's frustrating." She sighed.

"Yes, it is. But I'm sure we'll get to the bottom of it."

She hung up the phone with pressure building in her chest. She'd been so certain the night before that Parker was the killer, but now, she had no idea what to think. She continued to make heart shaped hazelnut milk chocolates, her mood dampened quite a bit. Just as she poured the chocolate into molds, Charlotte arrived.

"Morning Ally." She walked in with a bright smile. "How are you this morning?"

"A little stressed to be honest. I just found out from Luke that Parker has an airtight alibi, and I'm pretty frustrated about that. We're almost out of milk for the hot chocolate, and I'm afraid to even call and check on the delivery." She sighed as she fiddled with her phone.

"Ugh, that is frustrating. He was such a good suspect. Maybe his alibi isn't as airtight as they think? And why are you afraid to call?" Charlotte set down her purse and checked on the milk supply. "Oh, yes you're right we're going to need more and fast."

"I am worried Isaac might think we told Harriet about the two boxes of chocolates."

"But we didn't, so we don't have to worry."

"How do you think Harriet knew that he bought two boxes?"

"She probably saw it on their credit card statement or something."

"I think he paid in cash." Ally bit into her bottom lip. "But I'm not sure." She paused, then looked over at her grandmother. "If he did pay in cash how could she know that he bought two boxes?"

"I'm not sure. But, Mrs. Bing did say she followed him around, right? Maybe she saw him buy the chocolates. Though if she did, I'm not sure why she would have been asking us to confirm it. Maybe she saw him give the other box of chocolates to someone else?" Her eyes widened. "That would explain why she was so enraged, because she already knew the truth, but she wanted us to confirm it. Not that he was having the affair but that he had the audacity to buy both boxes of chocolates at once. I hate to say this, Ally, but I think that we need to pay a visit to Harriet."

"Why do you say that?" Ally studied her grandmother as she tried to fit whatever pieces together she could.

"Because I have a feeling she knows a lot more

about this situation than she is letting on. She came into our shop yesterday for a reason. She didn't just want confirmation, she wanted witnesses, people to observe and share her pain. I have a feeling that she knows exactly who Isaac was having an affair with, and if she's angry enough she may cause harm to that person. If we don't figure out who it is and warn her, that woman, whoever she is, could be in a lot of danger."

"Oh, Mee-Maw, I hadn't even thought of that." Ally sighed and shook her head. "Maybe we should have tried to cover up for him."

"Nothing we did would have made a difference. She already knew. She just wanted an audience. And someone that wants that kind of attention is usually no stranger to drama. None of this is your fault, or my fault. This is about Isaac and Harriet. Honestly, we don't even know for sure if he was having an affair."

"Well, if we don't know now, we might be about to find out." Ally tilted her head towards the side where the milk truck could be seen through the window.

"Just keep in mind, no matter how he behaves none of this is really our business. We find out what we can, and if possible, the name of the person he gave the chocolates to. That way we can at least try to warn her. Okay?" She met Ally's eyes.

"Okay." Ally rubbed her hands together nervously. She walked towards the door to open it for Isaac and prepared herself for his anger or accusations. When she pulled it open, she found Marlo with a cart full of milk crates.

The sight of him made her draw a sharp breath. She knew he might have a history of criminal behavior, and after the way he'd acted the last time she spoke to him she wasn't sure what to expect.

"I'm sorry, I didn't mean to scare you." He coughed, then leaned on the handle of the cart. "I have your milk for today."

"It's okay, I was just expecting Isaac." She stared at him for a long moment uncertain if she wanted to let him inside. "Where is he?"

"Don't know. He just didn't show up today. Milk needed to be delivered. Supervisor said I should do it. Here I am. You want the milk?" He shrugged as he looked into her eyes. "If not, I'll take it back."

"Yes, we want the milk." She stepped away from the door and held it open so that he could roll the crates through. He nodded to Charlotte as he headed past her with the crates.

"Good morning." She nodded to him in return.

As he disappeared into the kitchen the two women exchanged glances. "What is he doing here?" Charlotte whispered.

"He said that Isaac didn't show up to work today. Do you think that Harriet did something to him?" Her eyes watered with the possibility. "What if she hurt him?"

"Okay, just take a breath. It may just be that he decided to find a new job, with the future of the farm so uncertain."

"Maybe." Ally lowered her eyes, then took a deep breath as her grandmother instructed. She became more determined than ever to find out the truth. When she pushed the door open and stepped into the kitchen Marlo had just moved the last crate off the cart. "Marlo, we need to talk."

"What?" He turned to look at her.

"I know you know something about what happened to Gladys. I understand why you're scared to tell the truth. You're afraid maybe you'll get in trouble, or get the wrong person angry at you. But I also know that Gladys took you in, when probably no one else would. Right? She knew about your history, and she still gave you a chance. Didn't she?" She searched his eyes.

"Yes." He frowned. "She did."

"Which means that she did you a big favor. You owe her for that. Are you really going to let someone get away with killing her?" She held her breath as she waited for his response.

"I don't know anything. Nothing." He glared at her. "I told the cops, I didn't see anything."

"Right, that's what you told them." Ally crossed her arms as her grandmother stepped up beside her. She put a restraining hand on Ally's shoulder.

"Marlo, what about the quad bikes? Did everyone on the farm use them?" Charlotte asked.

"Lots of people used them. I used them every day." He pursed his lips.

"What about when there is a problem with them? Were there any crashes before?" Charlotte let her hand fall back to her side.

"No, they were always in good shape. Parker, he's a mechanic, he'd check them over every month."

"Parker did?" She studied him closely. "Was there one quad bike that Gladys used more often than the others?"

"No, she just grabbed whatever one was available." He frowned as he looked down at his feet.

"Marlo, you can tell me if there's something on your mind. Just tell me what it is you're hiding."

130

"I have to go. I have other deliveries to make." He grabbed the cart and wheeled it past both of them towards the door. Ally stared after him, certain that he was leaving something out.

"He knows something, Mee-Maw. I'm going to find out what it is."

"Be careful when you're around him, Ally, he seems really unpredictable."

"Yes, he does." She narrowed her eyes.

CHAPTER 12

The day was busy, and the custom hot chocolate was one of the most popular choices. It was difficult to keep up at a few points, but they managed to fill every order with very little time for breaks. At closing time, Ally rushed to the door to lock it. However, a familiar face appeared right outside the door with big eyes and pouted lips.

"Mrs. Bing." Ally smiled as she pulled open the door. "We're closed, you know?"

"Yes, I know it's an early closing day. I'm so sorry, I was running behind on my errands, but I am just dying for some cherry cordials. Could I just buy one box please?"

"Sure." Ally held the door open for her, but she locked it behind her. She knew if they got another crowd of customers inside they might end up being open later, and they had plans to visit Harriet as soon as they could.

"Thank you so much. You're always so kind. I wish people could have the same pleasant demeanor as you." She sighed as she walked up to the counter.

"Oh, I'm not always pleasant, trust me." Ally laughed as she followed her to the counter, then walked around it to get the chocolates. "Mee-Maw, Mrs. Bing is here!" She shouted towards the back where she knew her grandmother was working on getting some chocolates ready for the next day.

"Hi, Mrs. Bing!" She called out from the back.

"Here you are, Mrs. Bing." Ally slid her the box of chocolates, then rang them up on the register. "Did you have a run-in with someone today?"

"Yes. And I know, she just lost her mother so I should be more understanding, but she was just so nasty." She scrunched up her nose as she handed Ally some cash.

"What do you mean? What happened?" Ally retrieved her change from the cash register and handed it over to her.

"I was at the grocery store, and she was there with her children, and just between you and me those kids are absolutely out of control. I know, I know, things are different these days, but they were running all over the place and screeching so loud it hurt my ears!" She huffed and opened her box of chocolates. Once she'd taken a bite, her eyes narrowed and she continued, "I simply asked her if she needed any help with the children, and apparently she took offense to that. She snapped at me and told me to mind my own business. Can you believe that?" She popped another chocolate into her mouth. "Her mother was right about her. She's an ornery little thing. She didn't seem the least bit bothered by her mother's death, and I know, I know, I'm not supposed to say things like that, but really." She huffed and popped a third chocolate into her mouth.

"I'm sorry that happened." Ally wondered if she'd actually eaten all three of the chocolates as her cheeks were puffed out a bit. "Did they not get along?"

"Not at all. Those two were like oil and water. I guess nothing has changed. I should be going." She grabbed her box of chocolates. "See you tomorrow, Ally."

"Have a good night, Mrs. Bing."

"I will now!" She waved the box through the air. Ally walked over with a smile to unlock the door for her, then locked it again behind her.

"Oh, I thought she wasn't going to leave." Charlotte laughed as she pulled her apron off and stepped behind the counter. "She had an awful lot to say about Bernice, hmm?"

"Yes, and honestly it made me consider that maybe we haven't looked into Bernice enough."

"What are you thinking?" Charlotte wiped down the counter as Ally shut down the register.

"Just that she might have had a reason to want her mother dead, too. If she really had such a strained relationship with her, maybe she decided to work with Parker to put an end to her." Her cheeks flushed. "I hate to even think it."

"Me too. But I think it's possible, too. I know we planned to go visit Harriet today, but I think we should shift our focus back on to Parker. He had access to the quad bikes, and stood to benefit the most from Gladys' death." Charlotte began to empty some of the sample trays as she spoke. "Maybe that alibi isn't rock solid. I'm sure that there's got to be some kind of cover-up going on at the farm. If we can get something, anything on him, then we might be able to steer the police investigation in the right direction."

"But what about Harriet and Isaac? We don't know if she did something to him, or if she plans to do something to the woman he is having an affair with. Or even if Harriet herself might be in danger." Ally tidied the boxes on the shelf. "We can't just leave that loose end flapping, can we?"

"No, we shouldn't. But there's only so much we'll find out from Harriet. She might not be willing to talk at all, at least not to us." She paused and looked over at Ally. "What about Luke? Do you think he would go have a talk with her?"

"I don't know, it probably has nothing to do with the murder investigation, and I'm sure that he's very busy. I can ask him, though. You're right, if she's going to talk to anyone it's going to be Luke." She pulled out her phone as she cleaned off the last of the counters. Instead of calling she sent him a long text with the information about Isaac not arriving for work. She'd already filled him in on their encounter with Harriet. After she sent the text, she turned back to her grandmother.

"I'll let you know when he gets back to me. Tomorrow I'm sure we're going to have a crowd to deal with. There are only two days until Valentine's Day."

"And tomorrow is Gladys' funeral." Charlotte carried the trays to the back of the store. Ally's heart sank at the revelation. She hadn't even thought about the funeral or when it might be. It was a reminder that they weren't just trying to solve a crime, they were trying to find a murderer.

As she did a final sweep of the shop, her cell phone buzzed. She checked it, and saw a text back from Luke.

"Mee-Maw, Luke says he'll stop by Isaac and Harriet's soon. He was planning on speaking to Isaac again, anyway."

"Great." Charlotte smiled as she stepped into the kitchen. "Hopefully he'll just find Isaac at home sick with a cold."

"Hopefully." Ally bit into her bottom lip. She grabbed her purse and keys. "I really feel like we're missing something. A visit to the farm will be good."

"Okay, I'll drive in case Luke calls you about what he finds at Isaac's."

"Deal." Ally handed the keys to her grandmother.

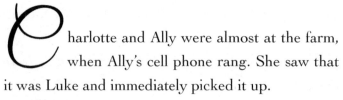

Charlotte and Ally were almost at the farm, when Ally's cell phone rang. She saw that it was Luke and immediately picked it up.

"Hi Luke."

"Do you have a minute?"

Ally glanced at her grandmother as she continued to drive towards the farm.

"Sure, what is it? Did you talk to Isaac?"

"I haven't been able to locate either of them, but there was also no sign of any distress at the house. Harriet apparently didn't show up for work today, either. I have 'be on the lookout' on both of their vehicles so I'm sure we'll locate them soon."

"I really appreciate it, Luke. I'm just a little worried about how Harriet might react since she suspects he is having an affair."

"I understand." He paused, then cleared his throat. "There's something else I want to tell you. I need to tell you this so you know what you are dealing with. But you have to keep it to yourself, got it?"

"Got it." She braced herself as she was certain it would be important information.

"We were able to identify the owner of the car in the other photograph that you sent. It turns out that he's a private detective. My best guess is that he was working with Rick to dig up dirt on Gladys."

"Here is a report I found about a business online that said they had the same experience. The company hired a private detective in an attempt to expose an affair the owner was having which was apparently just a rumor. They did it in order to ruin her business so that they could purchase it. She claims that the information was fabricated. I think that might have been what the detective was hired to do." She sighed. "I bet he didn't find anything about Gladys though, she was such a loner."

"Maybe not, but that doesn't mean that the private detective is innocent in all of this. It's possible that Gladys caught him."

"Well, you know about the police report now don't you, about her suspecting she had a stalker?"

"Yes, Errol flagged it for me, so I saw it. I can't believe it got overlooked in the first place. Parker being involved makes me even more suspicious of him. Something is really fishy here, and I intend to get to the bottom of it. But Ally, you've got to back off a bit. If this man, Oscar Hanso, is involved in the murder he could have shifted from investigator to hired gun, and his goal will be to get rid of anyone that gets too close. I don't want you in the crossfire. Understand?"

"Luke, we're getting so close and—"

"Ally." His voice grew almost stern. She knew he was always careful about not being too forceful, but she could tell from the edge in his voice that his patience was growing thin. "I mean it. If you and Charlotte insist on figuring out this situation with Isaac and Harriet so that you can help them, fine, but when it comes to the private detective, and Rick, I need you to stay clear. If they are involved in Gladys' death anything you do could taint the investigation. Okay?"

"Okay." She was reluctant to agree, but she knew he wouldn't accept anything less. She also knew that he was right. If she did something to harm the case he was trying to build against Rick, and perhaps the entire company, then it would be torn apart by their high priced lawyers and Gladys' murderer might just get away with it. As much as she didn't like it, she had to face the fact that she could only investigate so much. After she hung up, her grandmother looked over at her.

"What did Luke have to say?" Charlotte pulled up to the driveway of the farm, but didn't turn in.

"He had some new information, and we've been handcuffed." She quirked a brow and frowned.

"Handcuffed?" Charlotte stared at her with wide eyes.

"He asked us to stay away from Rick, and the other man he met with at the farm, Oscar Hanso, who is a private detective. I think he really believes that the company caused Gladys' death. He's concerned that any interference might cause damage to the case he's building against them." She sighed. "I know he's not wrong, Mee-Maw, so why does it feel like I've just been sent to the corner?"

"The hard part is, as much as Luke cares about you, he still has to do his job as a detective, and it's important that we both let him do that. Otherwise he could be in danger of losing it."

"I do know that, and his job is so important. I don't want to do anything to put it in jeopardy." She frowned as she looked out through the windshield. "Good thing he didn't say anything about not going to the farm. We're not here to speak to Rick or Oscar, we're here to speak to Parker. If we can find something that puts a hole in his alibi, then Luke can take a deeper look at him."

"Let's see what we can find out." Charlotte turned down the driveway, then continued past the house. "If Parker is still here, he'll be in the office." She parked in a small parking lot not far from the house. It faced a trailer that served as Gladys' office.

Ally noticed right away that there was a man standing near the trailer. She recognized him, though didn't know his name. He walked towards the car as they stepped out of it.

"Can I help you?" He looked between the two of them.

"We're looking for Parker." Ally stepped in front of her grandmother and gazed at him with squinted eyes. "Is he here?"

"I'm the farm supervisor. Chuck." He eyed them both again. "Why are you looking for Parker?"

"We just have a few questions for him." Charlotte offered a friendly smile. "We're customers."

"Ah." He studied her for a moment. "Do you have an appointment?"

"No, but we won't take long, we just need a few minutes." Ally shrugged. "Any chance you can find him for us?"

"He's not here right now. He should be back in an hour or so." The man adjusted his hat, then glanced over his shoulder. "I've got to get back to the cows. Anything else you need?"

"No, nothing." Charlotte frowned. "Wait, can I ask you a question?"

"Sure." He paused and looked towards her.

"Do you know what's happening with the farm? Did the sale go through?"

"Yes. It's going to change hands tomorrow, after the funeral." He shook his head. "Seems a little cruel to me to do it on the day of her funeral, but that's how business goes I guess."

Ally stared after him as he walked off. "So Bernice signed the papers?" She sighed.

"It looks that way." Charlotte pursed her lips. "Honestly, I hope that Gladys can't see any of this from wherever she is."

"Me, too." Ally glanced towards the office. "It looks empty. Maybe we should have a look inside?"

"That sounds like a good idea to me." Charlotte glanced around. "I don't see anyone else nearby. Let's see if the door is unlocked." She walked up to the door and tried the knob. It turned easily in her hand. "It's not locked." She looked over her shoulder again to be sure that no one was approaching. "Let's see what we can find."

Ally nodded as she stepped in behind her. Charlotte went straight to the desk and began to scan over some papers. Ally scanned the office. It was a little cluttered, with an assortment of farm supplies and stacks of file boxes. It looked as if the police had already searched the place as there was fingerprint dust on the windowsill and counters. She didn't think they'd find anything unusual if the police had already dug through it all, but still she searched.

After a few moments she took a step back and looked at the office as a whole.

"Nothing." Charlotte sighed as she set down a stack of papers. "Just business paperwork, and honestly I don't know if I'd even know if anything was odd. I've never run a farm before."

"Mee-Maw!" Ally gasped as she stared past her at the top of a filing cabinet.

"What?" Charlotte gazed at her with wide eyes. "Is someone coming?"

"No, Mee-Maw look!" She pointed over her shoulder at the filing cabinet. On the top of it was a box of chocolates and a hot chocolate container from Charlotte's Chocolate Heaven. The packaging was unmistakable.

"Oh!" Charlotte shrugged as she glanced at it. "I'd guess someone gave it to her. I don't remember her coming in to buy any."

"No, she didn't." Ally walked over to the box and the container. "This is one of the boxes of chocolates that Isaac bought. I know, because you told me that he asked for two flavors and this was one of them. I think it was the only almond and toffee hot chocolate we've sold. Did you sell any others?"

"No." Charlotte shook her head.

"That means he gave the other, cherry cordial, to his wife." Her stomach twisted with fear. "Oh, Mee-Maw, I think we know who he was having an affair with."

"Gladys?" Charlotte grabbed on to the desk to steady herself. "I never would have expected that. She was always so standoffish and distant. Honestly, it never crossed my mind that she might be interested in romance."

"Well, whether she was interested or not, Isaac sure was." She held the hot chocolate container, using the edge of her shirt to cover her fingertips and read the label. If the police had overlooked the box and container they might not have tested it for fingerprints. "Yes, just as I suspected, this is the hot chocolate he bought. There's no question in my mind that he's the one who gave her these." She frowned as she looked into her grandmother's eyes. "He was either in love with, or having an affair with Gladys, or both."

"No wonder he was so upset when he came into the shop." Charlotte pressed her fingertips to her lips as she recalled how distraught he was. Outside, the rumble of a motor drew her attention. "Ally, we have to get out of here, fast. That doesn't sound far off."

CHAPTER 13

*T*he roar of the motor bounced off the walls of the small space. For a split-second Ally considered that it might be Gladys, haunting her favorite place. But that notion faded as the sound dug into her ears. There wasn't anything supernatural about it. A ripple of almost overpowering fear rushed over her. Whoever it was, was about to catch them in Gladys' office, a place they had no right or permission to be.

"I'm right behind you!" Ally eased the lid back down on the chocolate box then followed her grandmother out of the office. As they stepped out, she saw a quad bike roaring up the trail. It skidded to a stop right in front of them, and Parker climbed off. She noticed that he wasn't wearing a helmet, despite

147

the fact that his own mother-in-law had just been killed in a quad bike crash.

"I was told you wanted to speak with me?" He crossed his arms as he looked between the two of them. "What were you doing in Gladys' office?"

"We thought there might be somewhere to sit inside." Ally pursed her lips. "We'd been waiting so long, we were getting tired."

"Good luck finding any space in that mess." He chuckled. "So what can I do for you?"

"We need to know about our milk supply. I keep hearing rumors about the farm being sold, but no one has let us know if we need to change suppliers." Charlotte narrowed her eyes as she studied him.

"Yes, the sale is going through tomorrow. Change of hands the next day."

"The same day as the funeral?" Ally stepped forward, her shoulders straight and her eyes sharp.

"So, you already know the details?" He looked between them. "But your milk supply shouldn't be affected."

"So, you really are selling the farm?" Charlotte asked.

"Yes, I'm doing what needs to be done."

"I had hoped that it was just a rumor." Charlotte shook her head, then passed her gaze around the farm. "Gladys would have hated this. She fought for her farm, didn't she? That's why there was bad blood between you."

"Excuse me?" He folded his arms across his chest as he focused all of his attention on her. "Are you implying that my mother-in-law and I had a difficult relationship? Do you really think that you know me well enough to make that kind of assumption?"

"No, honestly, I don't. And I didn't know Gladys that well either. But I do know that she loved this farm, and that she would have done anything to save it." She gazed right back at him, unaffected by his stern attitude.

"Not everything can be saved. Nor should it." He glanced past her, at Ally. "I'm sure that you will make an acceptable deal with the new owners or be able to find someone else to supply your milk. As of now, I'm requesting that both of you leave this property, and do not return. Understand?" His eyes hung on Ally with added pressure of authority. "I don't want to have to involve Detective Elm in all of this, but I will."

She narrowed her eyes but sealed her lips tightly. She knew that anything she said at this point could be used against her, or even against Luke. But she was still tempted to ask more.

"Let's go, Ally." Her grandmother slipped her arm through Ally's and steered her back towards the car.

"But I wanted to ask him some more questions." Ally frowned as they reached the car. "He was right on the edge. If we pushed just a little harder, he would have admitted to something."

"Or he would have had us both arrested for harassment and filed a complaint against Luke. Trust me, Ally, that man is far more conniving than he looks." She shivered as she climbed into the car beside her.

"We have to figure out whether Bernice was involved in all of this. I'm honestly not ready to rule out Parker as the killer."

"And now we know that Harriet might have had a motive as well. So, either Bernice helped Parker cover up for his involvement, or was involved herself, or Harriet took care of her competition."

"Or, Luke was right and Rick and Oscar conspired to kill Gladys." Ally shook her head. "Honestly, the deeper we dig the more reasons we find for Gladys to be murdered, and the less certainty we have about who did it."

"You're right. A good night's sleep might give us some clarity."

"You keep the car. I want to pick up the van from the shop." Ally settled in the car. "I might have one more stop to make." She fired off a text to Luke.

I have new information. Can I stop by?

By the time they arrived at the shop, Luke had replied.

Yes. Asap.

The short text made her feel a little uneasy. She guessed he was just very busy, but her instincts told her there might be something more to it. After saying goodbye to her grandmother, she settled into the van and drove towards the police station. As she approached she tried to plan out what she would say. She had no way to prove that the box of chocolates that Gladys had, came from Isaac. She had no way of knowing whether she and Isaac were having an affair or just very good friends, but she was certain that finding the box of chocolates there was important.

When she parked outside the police station the parking lot was mostly empty. Shift change had just occurred, and she knew that the late shift was sparser. But Luke was clearly still there, and no matter what he was dealing with he had made sure to make time for her, which was very kind of him. She just hoped that the information she had for him would make the impact she wanted it to. As it looked, he might be working overtime for the next month as he tried to solve this murder. If she could give him the clue that cracked the case they might be able to have a little more time together. There were so many reasons she wanted Gladys' death solved, but the most important one was to restore a sense of safety to the community. No one wanted to believe that a murderer was living among them, and unless they found out who did it, that could be the case for years to come. Everyone would be a little suspicious of each other as long as an unsolved crime lingered.

When Ally stepped into the police station she found the lobby to be just as empty as the parking lot, while an officer snoozed at the front desk. She nodded to a few other officers as she made her way back towards Luke's desk. She visited often enough that they recognized her and didn't question why she was there. She could see Luke before he could notice her, as his back was to her. A very tense back. His desk phone was pressed to his ear. She soundlessly walked up to the desk, not wanting to interrupt. However, when he looked up at her she thought about turning right around and walking out. That look. It made her tense immediately. It was both betrayal and accusation, wrapped up in a grimace that she rarely saw on the very patient man. Her lips parted as he slammed the phone back down in the cradle, but before she could say a word, he locked his eyes to hers and took a deep breath.

"Ally, were you just out at Bloomdale farm?" His tone was calm, too calm, despite the flush in his cheeks.

"Yes, I was just there." Her voice wavered some as she wondered what had him so upset. "What's going on, Luke?"

"Parker just filed a complaint against me. He is claiming that I gave out personal information." He locked his eyes to hers. "Any reason why he might have done that?"

Her heart sank. She was certain that the complaint was unfounded, but she also knew that the only reason Parker filed it was because she and Charlotte had visited the farm.

"Honestly, I didn't tell him any personal information of any kind. I don't know why he would say that." She bit into her bottom lip.

"But you did speak to him?" He stood up from the desk and walked around it to her.

"Yes, I did." Her cheeks burned as her heart slammed against her chest. Had she said something that made the complaint valid? She didn't think so.

"What did you say?" He perched on the edge of the front of his desk, his eyes still settled to hers, and his voice still calm, but strained.

"I just asked him about the milk supply, when the farm was closing." She narrowed her eyes as she recalled the conversation. "Things may have gotten a little heated when Mee-Maw said that Gladys wouldn't have wanted to sell the farm. But they didn't get very heated, and I didn't repeat any information that you shared with me."

"He seems to think that you did." He folded his arms and stared at her. "But of course, I trust your word over his. Which means he is just interested in making trouble for me. Any reason he might want to do that?"

"Maybe we got a little too close for comfort?" She frowned as she thought back over the conversation. "It is pretty heartless of him to have the sale of the farm finalized on the day of the funeral."

"Maybe, but it's not illegal." He ran a hand across his forehead and took another deep breath.

"I'm sorry if I did anything to get you into trouble, Luke, I certainly didn't mean to." She reached for his hands. His long, warm fingers wrapped around hers as he met her eyes again.

"Don't worry about it. It's nothing. It'll be dismissed once this case is solved." He gave her hand a squeeze. "Now, what is the information you had to share with me?"

"We found something." She swallowed back her guilt and focused on giving him the information. "We found a box of chocolates and an empty container of hot chocolate in Gladys' office."

"In her office?" He raised an eyebrow as he continued to hold on to her hand. "And what were you doing in her office?"

"Luke, that's not the point, the chocolates—"

"It is the point. It's the point if you didn't have permission to be there and decided to just let yourself in. Parker could have you charged for that." He frowned.

"The door wasn't locked." Her eyes widened innocently.

"That doesn't always make a difference. You were on his property and entered a private building. That's a crime." He ran his hand back through his hair. "Normally. I wouldn't be concerned about it, but Parker seems to be chomping at the bit to cause us trouble." He cupped her cheek with his hand and stared hard into her eyes. "I know that you want to help, and I know that you have very good instincts, but this case is very difficult. I need you to understand that this is my job, this is what I love. I hope that you will respect that and not put it at risk."

"I would never put it at risk, Luke, I promise. But I think I know who the killer is."

"What?" His eyes widened. "Why didn't you just say so?"

"I've been trying to!" She frowned as she grabbed his hand and held it tightly in her own. "Isaac was having an affair with Gladys, at least we think he was. He bought two boxes of chocolates from our shop, one for his wife, and we think we found the other in Gladys' office."

"And Harriet was furious." His eyes narrowed as he put two and two together. "That does give her motive. What kind of proof do you have?"

"Well, uh, none yet." She lowered her eyes. "But it must have been her, don't you think?" When she looked back up at him she saw the strain in his expression.

"So, what you have is a hunch?" He raised an eyebrow and pursed his lips in the same moment. She knew that look. It meant he was trying to be patient with her. She hated to see that look.

"Okay, yes, but it's a good one. Right?"

"Yes, a good one." He pulled away from her and headed for the door. "I have to go. But I'll look into it." He paused in the hallway, and turned back to look at her. "Stay off the Bloomdale property, understand?"

Ally noticed a few of the other officer's glance in her direction. With her teeth clenched she nodded. An instant later he was gone through the door. She knew that when Luke was on a case he was hyper-focused and didn't like to be distracted. She headed through the door. As she stepped outside the cold air hit her like a slap in the face. In that moment she realized that she might just be doing the same thing. She'd decided that the killer was Harriet, but there were still plenty of other suspects that had motive, not the least of which was Parker, with his smug attitude about selling the farm. She thought of Bernice, home alone with her kids, and how deter-mined she was not to sell the farm. What had Parker done to her to convince her that she should sell?

As she marched to the van her thoughts became a parade of conversations. Marlo, Parker, Harriet, Bernice, and even Isaac. He had seemed like such a nice guy to her, and yet it appeared as if he was living a double life. There were so many people that could have been involved in Gladys' death, and not many friends to defend her honor.

Once in the van she texted her grandmother.

Can we meet and talk?

As she started the van she received a text in return.

I'll meet you at the cottage.

Ally was relieved to see that as she knew she owed Arnold and Peaches some attention and they would both be thrilled to see Charlotte. She wanted to play with them more. Arnold needed his exercise and they both needed to have fun.

When Ally pulled up to the cottage she noticed a car in the driveway. Her heart skipped a beat as she didn't recognize it. Why would someone she didn't know be parked in her driveway? She parked in front of the cottage, and stepped out of the van. She noticed that the front door of the cottage was slightly open. Alarms rang out in her mind as she realized that someone could have broken in. Her first instinct was to call Luke, but he was so busy, she didn't want to bother him if it turned out to be nothing. Instead, she soundlessly approached the house. As she listened outside the door she heard Arnold snorting and squealing. Was someone hurting him? She summoned all her strength as she slammed the front door open and shouted in the same moment.

"Get away from him!"

A figure in the living room, jumped, and spun around to face her. Her heart dropped as she recognized the man who stood, uninvited, in her home.

CHAPTER 14

"*M*arlo! What are you doing here?" Ally lingered near the front door, ready to run if she needed to.

"We were just playing, I didn't hurt him." He smiled and patted the top of the pig's head. Arnold snorted, and brushed his head against the man's palm. He was clearly not frightened, or harmed. His snorts and squeals were of excitement that someone was paying attention to him, not fear.

"Why are you in my house?" She pulled her phone out of her pocket. "I've already called the police."

"Oh, you did?" His friendly expression faded into panic. "I'm sorry I didn't mean to do anything wrong. It's just that the pig was in the front yard, and I was afraid he might get hurt or run away, and the door was open, and I — "

"Marlo, wait a minute." She took a step closer to him. "What do you mean he was in the front yard?"

"I came by to speak to you, but I saw the pig out there and I thought he might get hurt. I just didn't want him to get hurt." He blinked as tears filled his eyes. "I don't want anyone to get hurt"

"Okay Marlo, just take a deep breath." She rested her hand on his shoulder and tried not to be swayed by the tears in his eyes. Was it all an act? One moment he seemed a bit manipulative and the next he appeared so innocent that she wondered if he might still be a child in his mind. "Arnold, that's his name, he's safe. But the door shouldn't have been open."

"It was when I got here. The cat was out, too." He looked down at Peaches as she wound her way through his legs. Ally was a bit shocked by how friendly the cat was to him. Then she realized what must have happened. Peaches was a genius at opening doors. She would swing on it until it opened. She almost always locked the deadbolt to make sure that the cat couldn't escape. But in her rush to get out the door she might have forgotten to lock it that morning. The two pets, who enjoyed having lots of time outside, probably decided they had enough of her inattention. Peaches set them both free so that they could have some fun.

"Ally, what's going on here?" Charlotte paused in the doorway. "Marlo?" She gasped.

"It's okay, Mee-Maw, it's okay." Ally lowered her hand from Marlo's shoulder. "He was only trying to help. Right Marlo?"

"Right." He sighed and wiped at his eyes. "I'm sorry. I keep making mistakes."

"It's all right, Marlo." She smiled at him as gently as she could. "Why don't you tell me what you came here to talk to me about?"

"It wasn't my fault." He looked into her eyes. "It wasn't."

"Okay, it wasn't. What wasn't?" Ally continued to study him with as much empathy as she could muster. Charlotte's hand slipped around her elbow. Ally could tell from the quiver in her touch that she was still concerned that Marlo could be dangerous.

"Gladys wasn't supposed to die. She shouldn't have. I don't know why all of this happened. But secrets. Secrets kill everyone."

"Secrets? Like what kind of secrets, Marlo?" Her tone became more insistent. "Did Gladys have secrets?"

"Yes. She did. She was supposed to be at a meeting, with Parker and Rick. But then Harriet showed up."

"Harriet?" Charlotte's voice grew sharp. "What was she doing there?"

"She was screaming at Gladys. She told her she knew everything, that she was going to pay." He shivered. "I didn't think she meant it."

"Harriet was there right before Gladys got on the quad bike?" Ally's eyes widened.

"Yes. I didn't tell anyone, because Harriet is so crazy. I thought she was going to hurt me. But everyone will think it's my fault. Everyone will think it was my fault. But it wasn't my fault."

"We know that, now." Charlotte nodded slowly. "Did Harriet say anything else while she was there?"

"No, just screaming. I don't like all of the screaming, so I don't listen to it." He lifted one shoulder in a shrug. "Can I play with the pig?"

"Sure. He needs some exercise anyway." Ally grabbed his harness and fastened it on, then led Marlo and Arnold outside. Not to be left behind, Peaches darted out after her. Charlotte lingered by the front door as Ally watched Marlo chase Arnold around.

"Ally, what happened here?" Charlotte pointed to some crumbled wood on the door frame.

"What do you mean?" Ally walked over to take a look. As her grandmother noted, the wood where the door latched was splintered and scraped. She stared at it for a long moment as she realized the assumption she made about her cat was wrong. Peaches hadn't swung on the handle until she managed to get the door open. She hadn't coerced Arnold into joining her for a romp around the neighborhood. She had likely been terrified as she heard someone outside the door prying it open. The thought made ice run through her veins. She'd been so quick to assume that Marlo was telling the truth, that he'd seen Arnold roaming and wanted to help him. Barely able to draw a breath, she spun on her heel.

"Marlo!" Her sharp tone made her grandmother's eyes widen. As Ally scanned the front yard she saw Arnold, and she saw Peaches chasing after him and batting at his loose harness leash. But Marlo was gone. His car was still in the driveway, but he was gone. "Marlo!" She ran to the edge of the yard and looked over the short fence into the street. There was no sign of him in either direction. Somehow, he had managed to slip away, right out from under her nose.

"Ally." Charlotte wrapped an arm around her shoulders. "Do you think he broke in?" She gazed at her with deep concern in her eyes.

"I don't know what else to think, Mee-Maw. He was certainly here for a reason." Her heartbeat quickened.

"Call Luke, he's going to want to know about this." Charlotte pursed her lips.

"No." Ally's voice was firm.

"No?" Charlotte stared at her. "Why not? Your home was broken into, Ally. Anything could have happened."

"No, I want to find out what happened here first. Luke is very busy, and I don't want to give him more reason to be frustrated with me." She shook her head. "I can handle this myself."

"I can tell you that if you don't tell him, he's going to be pretty frustrated with you. I would be." Charlotte squinted at her. "What is the real reason you don't want to tell him?"

"I don't want him to arrest Marlo." She looked over at her grandmother. "I think Marlo might lead us to the truth, and if he locks Marlo up, he won't have the chance. The funeral is tomorrow morning. I want to see who Marlo interacts with."

"Do you think we should go?" Charlotte continued to survey the street and nearby houses. She was on high alert for anything that looked suspicious.

"I think we have to. It's not at the farm, so we have every right to attend. But I will follow your lead on this, Mee-Maw, what do you think?" She pushed the front door closed, and watched as more of the wood splintered.

"We'll be there." Charlotte scowled at the door frame. "I'm betting that whoever did this will be there, too, and I won't let them think that we've been intimidated by their behavior."

"Good." Ally nodded then looked over at her. "I think we've had enough adventure for today." She gathered the animals and herded them inside.

"Are you planning on staying here?" Charlotte frowned. "I don't think that's safe."

"I don't want to be intimidated. Don't worry, the deadbolt still works." Ally showed her that the lock would still engage. "Unfortunately, I think I forgot to lock it." Her cheeks flushed as she knew that was a mistake that she shouldn't have made.

"It's okay, Ally." Charlotte kissed her cheek. "Be

safe. I'll pick you up first thing in the morning. I think you should leave the van out front, so it looks like someone's home."

"Good idea."

Ally gave her a hug, then stepped inside the cottage. Her two hungry friends were not so pleased with her as she put their dinner down far too late in the evening.

"Sorry guys, I've been a little distracted." Ally crouched down to pet both of them. "I'm sorry for all of the craziness. But hopefully it will be over soon."

~

As Ally settled into bed that night, her thoughts were on Luke. He was always so kind to her, but sometimes she wondered what he really felt. She knew that he loved her, he wasn't shy about saying or showing that, but that didn't mean that he didn't get frustrated with her. Her grandmother was probably right, that he would be annoyed she hadn't told him about the break-in. However, she needed to figure things out before he reacted. If he thought she was in any danger he would do everything in his power to protect her.

She felt as if Marlo was her only link to the truth, and with him behind bars, she would not be able to get any more information out of him. Peaches snuggled up close to her. She ran her fingers through the cat's soft fur and closed her eyes.

"What happened today, baby? I know that someone scared you. I only wish that you could tell me who." She recalled the way that Peaches had wound around Marlo's legs. Peaches had great instincts when it came to people. More than once Peaches had hissed or swatted at someone that Ally thought was a friend and had turned out to be someone that she shouldn't trust. However, she hadn't acted that way with Marlo at all. Instead she acted as if she was friendly with him, even fond of him, when she'd never seen him before. Her eyes opened and she gazed at her cat.

"Did someone else break in, Peaches?" She narrowed her eyes. "It wasn't Marlo, was it?" Her thoughts spun as she considered that Marlo had been telling the truth. Maybe Arnold had been roaming the front yard, because whoever broke in, didn't close the door properly. Maybe Marlo did have good intentions when he stopped at the house to make sure the pig got back inside. But if that was the case, then who had broken in? The question pressed on her mind so heavily that she couldn't relax enough to fall asleep.

Parker? She doubted that he would be bold enough to do that. But she did know one person that might be. He would have enough experience sneaking around and breaking in not to think twice about breaking into the cottage. Oscar. The private detective and possibly a hired assassin. She closed her eyes and pictured the man at her front door. She thought about him glancing over his shoulder, checking to be sure that no one else was around, then prying his way into her home. The image made her skin crawl. But maybe it was just a fantasy. She had no proof that it had been Oscar that broke in. In fact, she couldn't be sure that whoever did break in was connected to the case at all. It could have been someone entirely different, who just wanted to break in to look for valuables. Of course she knew that there were no valuables for anyone to find in the cottage. What items of worth she did have were stored in a safe deposit box at the bank. She didn't keep cash around, and had barely any jewelry to speak of, and what pieces she had were mostly costume.

As she began reviewing the contents of the cottage in her mind, she fell asleep.

CHAPTER 15

*W*hen Ally woke the next morning, the weight of the day before was still on her shoulders. She did her best to wash it off in the shower, but it still clung as she got dressed. It was hard to choose what to wear, as a funeral was never straightforward for her. Was it a celebration of life, a grief-stricken moment? Should she wear something bright, or something dark and dreary? She chose something in the middle, then walked into the kitchen to feed the pets.

As soon as Ally set foot in the kitchen, both came scampering towards her. Well, more accurately one scampered, and one lumbered with accompanying snorts. It was rather amusing to see Arnold in the morning. He still had droopy eyes as if he might just curl up and fall back to sleep, but his snorts indicated he was more than ready for breakfast. Peaches on the other hand, would jump up onto the counter and prowl back and forth, eagerly meowing just in case Ally forgot that she was there. It was somewhat entertaining, but could also be annoying at times. Luckily, that morning, Ally was in the mood for a little meowing. She even meowed back. It felt good to be surrounded by friends when she was faced with such a sobering experience.

After Ally gave the pets their food she put together a small breakfast for herself and made coffee to share with her grandmother. As if she could smell it from Freely Lakes, Charlotte texted to let her know that she was on the way. Ally smiled to herself as she thought of her grandmother. She was one of the strongest women she knew, and each day she discovered something more fascinating about her. As much as she wanted to emulate her, she felt as if she could never quite measure up. Although Charlotte would never make her feel that way. In fact, she'd adored Ally since the day she was born, and never once questioned her choices.

Now and then she would give her a gentle reminder of what turns life could take, but other than that she'd stood back and let Ally steer her life the way she chose. That didn't always work out for the best, but in the end, her grandmother was always there to support her when she needed it. She only hoped that she could do the same for her. When she heard a light beep in front of the house she gathered two travel mugs of coffee and headed out the door. Once she settled in the passenger side she handed over a mug to her grandmother.

"Enjoy, it's still hot."

"Thanks so much for this." She smiled as she looked over at her. "You look nice."

"Thank you, so do you. I like the color." Ally smiled as she swept her gaze over her grandmother's dark rose ensemble. It wasn't exactly dark, and yet it wasn't exactly cheerful either, it was a nice combination. On the way to the funeral home, Ally's stomach twisted with anxiety. Would it be disruptive for them to be there? Would Parker try to kick them out? She sent a quick text to Luke to see if he would be there. By the time they reached the funeral home she still hadn't received an answer. The parking lot was packed, and although the funeral home was quite large, there were many people standing around outside the building. Charlotte and Ally walked through the crowd, greeting each person as they went. Many faces were familiar with only a few strangers that might have been distant relations or friends from out of town.

When they reached the door, Bernice and Parker stood in the doorway with the three children a few paces away. While Bernice and Parker both wore sullen expressions, the children were focused on the devices in their hands and giggling and poking at each other. Instead of being annoyed Ally was rather inspired by their playful display. It was difficult to say goodbye to a loved one, but the kids couldn't be bothered by it. Either they were too young to understand loss, or they just hadn't been very close to their grandmother. Maybe it was possible that Gladys simply didn't like children or didn't have the time for them. Ally thrust out her hand to Bernice.

"I'm very sorry for your loss."

"Thank you." Bernice met her eyes with a small smile. "I'm sure Mother would have been touched that you are here."

"Please, if there's anything you need, just let us know." Charlotte touched the back of her hand, then passed a brief glance towards Parker. "I know this must be a difficult time for all of you."

"The seats are filling up." Parker tilted his head

towards the interior of the funeral home. "Best to get one now."

It seemed like a rather odd statement to make in response, but Ally decided to ignore it. Everyone grieved in a different way. She and her grandmother made their way to the back row of seats.

The funeral home offered services despite not being a church. Ally thought it was a fine way to serve people who might not have been very religious. She also knew that it was part of a package deal that came with a casket and a grave stone. She pushed that thought from her mind and focused on the minister at the front of the crowd. Within minutes the service began. Ally checked her phone one last time, she still hadn't received a text back from Luke, then she turned it off. As she listened to the minister's words, she scanned the room. She saw no sign of Harriet or Isaac. Marlo didn't appear to be there either. She was a little disappointed that he wasn't as she had hoped that he would point her in the right direction.

Only a few moments into the service, the doors flung open, and a man stepped inside. At first Ally thought it was the supervisor from the farm, then she realized it was Marlo. He settled into a seat not far from them, and began to rock back and forth in his chair. Ally glanced at her grandmother, then gave her a slight nudge with her elbow. Charlotte turned to look and saw Marlo as well. Just as she was about to whisper to Ally, Marlo stood up and began to walk towards the front of the room. A few gasps could be heard throughout as he marched right up to the minister. He fell down on his knees before the man, and cried out so loudly that everyone in the room could hear.

"Please, I have a confession to make."

Several people, including Charlotte and Ally, stood up from their seats to stare at the man on his knees.

"All right, son, just calm down." The minister's face grew beet red, and he searched the audience for someone to help him with the strange man.

"What is he doing?" Ally whispered to Charlotte. "Do you think he intends to confess to Gladys' murder?"

"Maybe." Charlotte gathered her skirt and made her way to the end of the aisle. As she approached Marlo, Ally was right behind her. Several other people had moved towards him.

"Marlo, what are you doing?" Ally stepped up behind him. "Are you okay?" She rested a hand on his shoulder.

"Don't touch me!" He moaned, and writhed as he remained on his knees. "I don't want anyone to stop me from telling the truth. It was my fault, she's dead because of me!"

"Just tell us." Charlotte's voice was soothing. "If you want to tell us, we are all here listening. Let it out, Marlo. Tell us what really happened."

"Enough." Parker stood up, his eyes narrowed and his jaw tense. "This is completely inappropriate. Marlo, you need to leave."

"Parker, please, let me speak." He gazed up at the man with tears streaming down his cheeks. "I'm so sorry, Parker. I didn't know any better. I just did what I was told."

"That's it." Parker grabbed him by the collar and pulled him to his feet. "You are leaving."

"Wait." Ally took Marlo's hand. "I'll walk him out. Right, Marlo? You and me? We can go see how Arnold's doing, okay?"

"Okay." Marlo's face crumpled with despair. "No one wants to listen to me."

"I know, Marlo, but I will." She patted the back of his hand. "It's okay, let's go take a walk."

"I don't care what you do, but get out of here." Parker pointed sharply towards the door. As Ally guided Marlo down the aisle, Charlotte followed after her. As soon as the trio stepped outside, someone closed and locked the door behind them. Charlotte frowned as she glanced back over her shoulder.

"I have a feeling we're not welcome to go back in, either."

"That's all right. The service wasn't much of an honor to Gladys, anyway." Ally shook her head. Then she turned her attention to Marlo. "Do you want to tell me, Marlo? I'm listening."

"Ally, she was a good woman. A woman that didn't deserve this. I shouldn't have let her take my quad bike."

"Why not?" She studied him. "Didn't she use it often?"

"No. She only used it that day because she was running late. I let her take it. I told her, go fast, you'll make it." He wiped at his eyes. "I told her, go fast."

"Marlo, you were riding the quad bike that day?" Charlotte stared into his eyes.

"Yes. I rode it out there to find her, because she was late for the meeting. She was supposed to meet with Rick and Parker. Parker was mad. He told me to go find her. So I did. I heard the screaming. Harriet was screaming at her. I parked the bike and followed the voices until I found them. But I was too scared to interrupt. So, I just waited."

"How long did you wait?" Ally raised an eyebrow as she looked at him. "A few minutes? An hour?"

"More than a few minutes, but not as much as an hour." He raised a finger in the air. "I can't be sure."

"Okay, you don't have to tell us right now, Marlo. But are you sure that the quad bike was working okay when you rode it out to the fields?" Charlotte searched his eyes. "You're certain there was no trouble with the brakes?"

"I'm certain." He nodded, then smiled at her. "I'm certain." His expression grew dreamy as he continued to stare at her.

"Marlo, can you tell me —"

Before Ally could finish her question, tires squealed in the parking lot behind her. She spun around to see Luke stepping out of his car. His eyes passed over her, and locked on Marlo.

"Marlo, I'm here to talk to you." He glanced back at Ally once, and held her eyes for a moment, then turned his attention back to Marlo. "Do you want to go for a ride with me?"

"I want to see the piggie." Marlo frowned.

"I told him we could take a walk with Arnold." Ally wondered if that was a mistake.

"That's all right, you can take Arnold for a walk later. Right now we need to talk, Marlo, okay? It's very important." He continued to stare hard at Marlo.

"Luke, he told me something that you should know." Ally stepped up close to him and murmured the information that Marlo had given her. "It sounds to me like Marlo was actually the target. How could anyone know that Gladys would climb on to the quad bike instead?"

"It's interesting." Luke shook his head slowly from side to side. "So, Gladys might not be the target. But, that may not be the case. Marlo is very easily influenced. It's possible that someone told him to say this. It could be a way of deflecting attention. I don't know, I've got a few irons in the fire."

"Be careful, Luke. Marlo can be a little unpredictable," Ally said quietly as she walked behind Marlo to Luke's car. "I would never have expected him to burst in and make a scene like that."

"It's bad timing." Luke nodded towards the funeral home. "Hopefully the rest of the service won't be interrupted." After he helped Marlo into the back of the car, he paused and glanced back at Ally. "Are you doing okay?"

"Yes, I'm fine." She took his hand and gave it a light squeeze. "What about you? Any sleep at all?"

"I'm sure I'll be sleeping soon." He placed a light kiss to her forehead. "Are you two opening the shop today?"

"Yes we are." Charlotte glanced at her watch. "We figured we'd wait until the service was over out of respect. But it's the day before Valentine's Day, we can't miss out on the sales."

"I'm sure that you'll have plenty of business, and it'll be nice for people to have somewhere to go after the service and enjoy some time together." He nodded to both of them. "I'll talk with you later." As he settled in the driver's seat, Ally waved to him. She wanted to ask a million questions. Had he found Isaac and Harriet? Did he know who might have pressured Marlo into saying things that weren't true? But she knew that if he wanted her to have the information he would have given it to her. At the moment she needed to focus on getting the shop open, as her grandmother had said, they needed the Valentine's Day sales.

CHAPTER 16

*A*fter Ally watched Luke drive Marlo away, she walked over to her grandmother.

"Should we head over to the shop?"

"Yes, that might be best. I don't think interrupting the service by trying to get back inside is a good idea."

"No, me either." Ally turned towards the parking lot. However, as she took a few steps she noticed two shadows near the side entrance of the funeral home. It only took her a second to recognize one of the people as Bernice. The other person was unmistakably Oscar. She grabbed her grandmother's hand.

"Mee-Maw, Bernice and Oscar are over there. What could they have to talk about? Oscar was

183

hired by Grainder, by Rick. Why would he be talking to Bernice?"

"I don't know, but they don't seem to be having a calm discussion. It must be important if she's outside instead of being inside the funeral home." Charlotte squinted in an attempt to get a better view. They were too far away to hear any of the conversation, but Oscar appeared to be rather agitated, while Bernice kept waving her hands and backing up from him.

"Let's try to get closer."

"Look, if we go over near that bush they shouldn't be able to see us." Ally led the way towards it. Just as they reached the bush, Bernice raised her voice.

"I have no idea what you're talking about! I don't owe you any money!"

Charlotte drew a sharp breath at that statement. She glanced at Ally, then looked back through the sparse leaves at Bernice and Oscar.

"I was hired to do a job, which I did, and now I want my payment. I know that you received your inheritance so you need to make it happen." He slapped the palm of his hand with the back of his other hand. "I expect payment right now."

"You're crazy. I never hired you to do anything. I don't have to pay you anything." She reached into her pocket and pulled out her phone. "I'm calling the police."

"Go ahead, sweetcheeks, and tell them how you had your sweet old mother followed around to try to get her declared unfit. I'm sure the police will love to hear all about that." He chuckled.

"Bernice!" Parker stepped out through the side door. "The service is almost over. The kids are looking for you." He grew silent as he saw who she was with. "What are you doing here?"

"What do you think?" He barked in return. "Rick took off without paying me, and I want payment. He said I could collect from you."

"Listen, this is not the time or the place for this."

"What is he talking about, Parker?" Bernice stared at him. "Did you hire him?"

"Not exactly." Parker cleared his throat. "Oscar, we can settle up later, all right? My wife is burying her mother."

"Sure, I can see a lot of tears are being shed." Oscar waved his hand. "I'll give you until six. But I have a flight out of here at ten tonight, and I expect to have my money when I get on the plane. If not,

185

I'll go to the cops and tell them what you hired me to do. I'm sure that will make the entire murder investigation that much more interesting. Don't you think?" He turned and walked off across the parking lot.

"Parker, what did you do?" Bernice shoved him hard on the shoulder. "What did you do?"

"Quiet, Bernice. Do you want the whole town to hear us?" He looked back towards the door that led to the funeral home, then turned back to her. "We'll talk about this after the service. We need to get back in there before one of the kids knocks over the casket."

Bernice continued to argue with him as she followed him back inside the building.

"Wow." Ally shook her head as she glanced at her grandmother. "So, Parker really did hire Oscar?"

"It sounds like he and Rick might have been in on it together. They probably teamed up to try to get Gladys declared unfit. Then the sale would have gone through very easily." She clucked her tongue. "I wonder if they took it so far as to kill her."

"They might have." Ally crossed her arms. "It sure sounds like they were determined to get the sale completed no matter what it took. But then, we just found out that it's likely that Marlo was the target, not Gladys. What motive could they have to kill Marlo?"

"Maybe he found out." Charlotte started to walk towards the car. "If he found out what they planned, maybe they decided they had to get rid of him first."

"Maybe." Ally sighed. "It still doesn't make sense to me, though." She settled in the passenger seat. She looked forward to the calming environment of the chocolate shop. "I can't believe that Oscar confronted her at her mother's funeral. What kind of person does that? Maybe he really did kill Gladys."

"It's possible. Everything's possible at this point. Which reminds me, we might have to find a new supplier for milk. We'll have to get some from the supermarket to hold us over until tomorrow."

"I'll take care of it, don't worry. Do you know where Jeff is taking you on your special Valentine's Day date tomorrow night?"

"Ugh." She waved her hand. "I don't know, and I don't think I'm going to go through with it."

"Mee-Maw, you have to. It will be fun." Ally looked over at her.

"I'm sure you're right." She pulled into the parking lot of the shop.

As they walked into the shop together, Ally felt a

rush of peace carry through her. No matter what was happening outside the shop, entering it was always like coming home, a form of comfort that couldn't truly be described.

"Mee-Maw, I'm going to head into the back and get some chocolate melting. Take your time, have some coffee, just relax a bit. Remember, you're going tomorrow!"

"I know, I know, tomorrow." She rolled her eyes. "At this point I'd rather just crawl into bed."

"Mee-Maw!" She gasped as she looked over her shoulder at her grandmother.

"Alone! Alone I meant!" Her cheeks burned bright red as she stumbled over her words. "I'm just exhausted." She laughed and shook her head. "I guess that came out wrong."

"Maybe it did, but it was funny." Ally grinned. "It's important for you to go, Mee-Maw, you need a little fun."

"It's just that I'm not in a celebrating mood. We just left Gladys' funeral, and we still don't know why she died. Now her farm is being sold, and who knows what will happen to it once a large company takes it over. I don't know, I guess I'm just feeling a little down about everything."

"I know how you feel." Ally wrapped her arms around her in a warm hug. "It's been a crazy few days, and it's not over, yet. I wish things would just calm down a bit so that we could enjoy spending some time together. No pressure, no investigating, just us. And by us, I mean Luke and Jeff, too."

"I agree with all of that. But it's hard for me to adjust to having someone around that wants to spend all of his time with me." She shrugged. "I've grown used to being alone, making my own choices, and not having to wade through the opinions of someone else."

"Sure, it can be frustrating at times. But having the company can be amazing, too. You have someone to laugh at a movie with, someone to share a great meal with, someone to go for a walk with under the stars." She cast a knowing smile in her direction.

"I told you that in confidence, you're not allowed to use it against me." Charlotte grinned.

"You care about him a lot, and he cares about you, too. It's normal to be afraid of losing that. If you admit that you are involved with him, then you have to be worried about things ending, right?"

"Maybe." She waved her hand. "Enough of this

chatter. We have work to do. If we don't get ready we're going to have to turn people away."

"You're right, Mee-Maw." Ally smiled. "Let's get started."

*a*s Ally stepped into the back of the shop her thoughts began to fill with excitement. Despite the fact that Gladys' death still weighed on her mind, she was eager to experience the day before Valentine's Day. She knew that it would be great for the shop, and the profits they made could go towards expanding their inventory. With these thoughts on her mind she turned on the burners and grabbed some chocolate to melt. An eerie sensation crept over her as she reached for a pot. A soft rustling sound made her heart stop.

As she held her breath, she heard the sound again. Was it a rat? Some other kind of unpleasant creature? Somehow she knew that it wasn't. Whatever it was, it made the same sound again, right behind her. She drew in a sharp breath to scream, without really knowing why, but before she could a strong hand clamped down over her mouth. It pressed so hard that her lips were crushed against her teeth. She struggled, but he had taken her by surprise, and she couldn't get any leverage.

"Sh." He whispered in her ear. "No need to upset Mee-Maw, right?"

In her panic, she didn't quite recognize the voice. She knew that it was familiar, but not who it belonged to. As the person pulled her towards the door, she realized she needed to do something, anything to draw attention to the fact that she was being taken. She kicked out her leg in an attempt to knock over some boxes, but he pulled her back before she could reach them. She screamed against his hand, but his grasp muffled her voice. The moment he pushed her through the back door, she knew exactly who had her. The milk truck was parked right by the door, with the back doors wide open and waiting for her. The person who held her was too tall to be Marlo. He shoved her into the back of the truck, and grabbed a large roll of tape. As she stared at him, with wide eyes, too stunned to move, Isaac slapped a thick piece of tape over her mouth. An instant later she flung her fist towards his face. He caught her wrist and pinned it behind her back. Within seconds her hands were bound, as were her legs. He gazed hard into her eyes.

"Behave." He latched her to the inside of the truck with a strong rope wound around her bent arms. She kicked her bound feet against the metal floor of the bottom of the truck. Despite the fact that she tried, the kicks did not create much of a commotion. Her heart sank as she wondered what he planned to do with her. Why would he take her in the first place? He slammed the doors shut.

～

*C*harlotte finished wiping down the counters, then headed to the kitchen to grab the sample trays. When she stepped in, she noticed a burning smell. Her heart jolted as she swept the kitchen in search of Ally.

"Ally? Did you leave the burner on?" She frowned as she turned the switch to off. The kitchen was quiet. After a moment, she checked the bathroom, but there was no sign of Ally. Her stomach twisted as she turned away from the bathroom. Her shoulder struck something solid and soft at the same time. She gasped as she recognized the sensation. She'd bumped into someone, but it wasn't Ally.

"Isaac?" She stared into his eyes as he stood over her. "How did you get in here?"

"Sh." He slapped some tape over her mouth, then spun her around and bound her by the wrists.

Charlotte tried to squirm out of his grasp, but he was quite skilled at what he was doing. As he pushed her towards the door she looked for anything that she could use to send out a signal that she was not safe. However, there was nothing. Her cell phone was in her purse out front, and she guessed that Ally had left hers behind as well. When she saw the delivery truck outside, her heart sank. No one would see them in the back of that. Isaac opened the double doors, then pushed her inside. She saw Ally curled up, not far from her, but she couldn't call out to her. As soon as the doors slammed shut, Charlotte struggled against the tape around her wrists. She didn't want to draw Isaac's attention to the slightly loose tape and have him wrap her wrists again. Despite the tape being a little loose, she couldn't get her wrists free. She knew if she could get close enough to Ally they could work together to set each other free.

Ally heard the doors open, then slam closed again. Her heart dropped as her worst fears came true. She had hoped that Isaac would leave her grandmother alone. Maybe he'd only wanted her, though she still didn't know why he wanted her. But there was her grandmother, just as bound as she was, and crawling towards her. She strained against the tape over her mouth, but no matter how hard she tried she couldn't force any words past.

Charlotte wriggled up beside her, just as the engine roared to life. She managed to get her fingers to the rope that had Ally bound to the side of the truck. As she tugged the rope free, she gazed at her granddaughter with fear. What were Isaac's intentions?

Once Ally's hands were free of the rope, Charlotte tugged at the tape that bound them. Ally winced as the heavy tape tugged at her skin. It took a few minutes, as the truck rolled along the road, but soon her wrists were completely free. She immediately tugged at the tape on Charlotte's wrists. She tried to be careful, but she could see the pain etched in her grandmother's face as she pulled it free. Once their hands were free they both reached for the tape on their mouth. Ally put her finger to her mouth, signaling that they needed to be quiet, just before she ripped the tape off her skin. She had to clench her teeth hard to keep from screaming in reaction to the tearing sensation.

Charlotte did the same, though a small moan did escape her lips. She braced herself for the truck to suddenly stop, but it didn't. If he'd heard the sound, Isaac wasn't concerned by it. Charlotte reached for Ally and pulled her close into a tight embrace. Then they went to work on the tape on their legs.

~

saac didn't speak, or turn the radio on. He just drove. Ally and Charlotte whispered to each other, afraid that he would figure out they were free if he overheard them

"Where do you think he's taking us?" Charlotte clutched Ally's hand.

"I don't know. I don't even know why he took us. Gladys must have rejected his advances, that must have been why he killed her." Ally grimaced as she thought of the horror that Gladys experienced. "Maybe he found out that we figured out who he gave that extra box of chocolates to."

"I never thought it was Isaac." Charlotte closed her eyes. "Not for a second."

"I didn't either." Ally bit into her bottom lip. "He seemed like such a nice man. Now, what do you think he's going to do with us?"

"If he's already killed once, then he's more likely to kill again." Her grim expression was an unusual one. Ally was used to her cheerful smiles, and always pleasant nature. She was usually the strong one. "So, we need to get out of this."

"We have to try to figure out where we are." Ally listened to the sound of the tires against the pavement. "We're definitely on a main road, not many bumps, and there are other cars, I can hear them."

"Yes." Charlotte crawled towards the back of the truck. She searched for a handle to open the back doors, but there was no latch that could be released. "We're going fast, too. Probably the highway."

"The highway." Ally sighed. "Which means he could be taking us anywhere." Just then the truck made a sharp turn, and both women slid across the truck. Ally gasped at the sudden movement. As the truck straightened back out again, she had to close her eyes to fight off dizziness. "He turned," she mumbled. "We were only on the highway for a few minutes. The first turn off is the one to the park."

"He's going to the park?" Charlotte narrowed her eyes. "Why would he be doing that?"

"I don't know." Ally's stomach twisted. "But I'm sure it's not good."

"Maybe he's taking us to someone else?" Charlotte sighed. "Maybe someone paid him to do this?"

"Maybe. But I think that it's possible he took us for another reason, I just can't figure out what it is."

The truck slowed. Suddenly, the road was bumpy, and Ally could hear the sound of gravel crunching under the wheels.

"Mee-Maw," she whispered, and met her eyes. "We're on the gravel path that winds around the lake. We're definitely at the park. Maybe there will be people nearby." Her heart lurched. "We should try to make as much noise as we can."

"But if we do, he'll know we're free." Charlotte frowned. "What if we're wrong, and we're not at the park?"

"The longer he has to drive, the less chance there is that we'll be found. I don't know, it might be our only chance, Mee-Maw. I know it's a risk, but if we just wait, who knows what out of the way place he'll take us to."

"You're right, Ally, but let's just wait a minute or two more. Let's listen, and see if we can hear any voices or any other cars."

Both women pressed their ears close to the back doors of the truck. It was hard to hear anything over the engine, and the gravel.

The crunch of the tires rolling across gravel gave way to a smooth sound. Ally's eyes widened as she tried to figure out exactly where they were. She knew the park well. She'd walked there many times with Arnold. What was around the gravel path that was smooth? It wasn't bumpy enough to be grass. A cold horror crept through her veins as she realized what it was. The boat ramp. It was the only smooth thing near the gravel. They had to be going down the boat ramp!

"Mee-Maw, he's going to drive the truck into the lake!" Sheer panic flooded through Ally as she realized they had no way out of the truck. Once it went into the water it would be impossible to escape. She knew that the lake was deep enough to swallow the truck, and there wouldn't be much chance of them surviving. If he was daring enough to drive straight into the lake, she guessed that there weren't many other people around to stop him. But there was only one thing they could do.

"No, he wouldn't, he couldn't!" Charlotte grasped at her chest for a moment. She took a deep breath, then nodded to Ally. "Let's make some noise!"

The two women began to scream. Ally kicked her feet against the back doors of the truck over, and over again, while Charlotte shrieked for help and banged on the wall of the truck. Despite how much they struggled, Ally felt as if it wasn't loud enough. The refrigerated truck was well-built, its walls were thick.

The truck continued to roll forward. Ally knew it was only a matter of seconds before they would be under water.

"Quiet down back there!" Isaac shouted from the front of the truck. "This is the way things have to be! I never planned it this way, but this is it! We're all going to come to an end together!"

Ally thought about how icy the water would be. It was February and the lake had just begun to thaw from the cold winter. There were still some ice patches in places. But mostly it was frigid water, from shore to shore. Even if the truck didn't fill completely with water right away the cold water would do just as much damage. She closed her eyes and grabbed her grandmother's hands. As she held them tight, she tried to figure out any way out of the truck. But without a crowbar, they could not get the back doors open, and that was the only exit.

"Please, Isaac!" She shouted towards the front of the truck. "Let us out! Please!"

She heard a screech of tires. The truck stopped

moving forward. She breathed such a deep sigh of relief that her entire body shook from it.

Charlotte laughed, and moaned at the same time.

Ally understood the mixture of emotions. Would the truck begin to move again?

CHAPTER 18

*A*lly heard shouts coming from outside the truck. They weren't clear enough for her to recognize any voices in particular, but she knew that there were other people outside the truck. That alone was enough to give her a second wind of energy. She screamed at the top of her lungs and kicked hard at the doors. Charlotte soon joined in.

"Let go, let go of me!" Isaac shouted from the front of the truck. "It's over! I have to do this! I have to!"

Ally grabbed her grandmother's hand and squeezed her eyes shut. She knew that things could go either way. If Isaac panicked he might plunge the truck into the lake. If he was pulled out of the truck, they might be set free within moments.

"It's going to be okay, Ally." Charlotte rubbed

her hand. "Listen, there are people out there. They are here to help us. Everything is going to be okay."

"You're right, Mee-Maw, I know you are." Ally still held her breath. When the doors to the truck opened, Ally was blinded by the sudden sunlight.

"Ally!"

The familiar voice brought tears to her eyes. "Luke, please get us out of here." She reached for him as she squinted against the sun. Errol climbed onto the truck and helped Charlotte off, as Luke wrapped his arms around Ally and held her close.

"You're safe now, sweetheart, I've got you. You're safe." He kissed her cheek, then her lips. Ally was a little surprised, as he didn't usually show affection in front of his colleagues.

"I love you, Luke."

"I love you, too. Are you okay?" He brushed her hair away from her face. "Did he hurt you?"

"No." She shook her head as she blinked back tears. "I'm okay. We're both okay. It was Isaac. I just can't believe it. Why would he do this?"

"That's what I'm going to find out." Luke helped her down off the truck, then headed straight for a small gathering of officers. Isaac was in the middle of them, cuffed, with tears rolling down his cheeks. Luke pushed past the other officers and glared straight at Isaac. "You made a terrible mistake, didn't you, Isaac?"

"Yes."

"You killed Gladys?"

"There's no way to fix it." Isaac shook his head. "I didn't want anyone to know the truth. I knew that Ally and Charlotte figured it out, because they sent you looking for me and my wife. I knew if they told the truth, then everyone would know what I'd done, and I just couldn't live with that."

"What did you do?" Luke took a step closer to him.

Charlotte and Ally huddled close together not far from the gathering of police officers. Neither had a coat on, and the cool air around them caused them to shiver, but their focus remained on Isaac.

"I loved her, I loved her more than I have ever loved anyone. We were going to be together. Then Marlo found out about our affair. I was scared he was going to squeal."

"So, you tried to kill him so he wouldn't tell your wife?" Luke asked.

"Well, yes." He grimaced. "But I was more worried that if he told everyone, or even if Gladys found out he knew about our relationship, she would call off our relationship. She was always so scared about someone finding out, she wanted to maintain her reputation. She often threatened to call it off because she was worried that if the community found out she was having an affair they would look down on her. I even offered to leave my wife, but she refused because then people would know. Gladys was the love of my life, I couldn't risk losing her." His eyes filled with tears as he looked down at his hands. He looked up as a few of the officers muttered. "I decided I would do something."

"What did you do?" Luke pressed.

"That day, I waited until Marlo went out into the fields. I didn't know why he was there. I waited until he left his quad bike. I cut the brake lines, so that he would crash. I figured, all of our troubles would be over. I never expected it to be Gladys that got on the quad bike! I never meant to kill her!" Fresh tears flowed down his cheeks as he took sharp anguished breaths. "I didn't mean to do it!"

"Enough." Luke nodded to Errol. "Take him into the station, we need to get a recorded statement."

As he turned back towards Ally and Charlotte he again offered a smile of relief.

"I'm so glad that you're both safe. I'm going to need statements from you, too. Do you want to ride with me?"

Ally slid her hand into his. She nodded, wordlessly. There was nowhere she felt safer than at Luke's side, and right then, she wanted more than anything to get as far away from the delivery truck, and the lake as she could.

"I almost feel sorry for him," Charlotte murmured as she joined them in the heated car. She rubbed her hands together and sighed as the heat flooded through her. "Almost."

"He meant to kill someone, he just didn't mean to kill her." Ally set her jaw. "I don't feel sorry for him at all. He meant to kill us, too, don't forget."

"How can I?" Charlotte shivered despite the warmth. "To think he was at our shop each morning and never once did I sense that he could be the murderer."

"What about Harriet?" Ally's eyes widened. "Did he hurt her? Did you find her, Luke?"

"I found her. Not long before I found you. She was never missing. She was visiting her sister while she made plans to file for divorce." He looked over at her. "You had good reason to be worried, just about the wrong spouse."

"How did you find us?" Charlotte sat forward in the backseat. "Not that I'm complaining."

"No, I hope not." Luke flashed her a smile. "Actually, you have Mrs. Bing to thank for that."

"Mrs. Bing?" Ally stared at him.

"She was waiting for you to open and noticed the truck squeal out from behind the shop. When she couldn't get hold of either of you she got worried and called me. We were able to trace the truck with local traffic cameras, unfortunately we couldn't catch up with it until it reached the park. I'm sorry we didn't get to it sooner." He frowned as he looked between both of them. "You two gave me a real scare."

"You?" Charlotte laughed. "You should have seen the two of us flopping around like fish in the back of that truck!"

~

*B*y the time all of the statements had been taken, and the paperwork filed, it was already late in the evening. Ally was relieved to get ready to head back to the cottage, but Luke caught her on the way towards the door.

"Wait a minute." He pulled her back to him. "Can you tell me something?"

"That I love you?" She smiled as she looked into his eyes.

"Well yes, that, but something else, too. Why was there evidence of a break-in at the cottage? I sent some officers to check it while we tracked the truck. Did you know about that?" He searched her eyes.

"Yes, I did." She frowned. "But I didn't want to bother you with it."

"That's ridiculous." He cupped her face with his hands. "You never bother me, understand? Of course I want to know if someone broke into your home. Isaac admitted that he broke in to see if he could find anything to use against you, to keep you quiet about the affair. But he didn't find anything."

"I'm sorry, Luke, I should have told you."

"Yes." He kissed her lightly on the lips. "I may be a detective, Ally, but I'm your partner first. We'll always be a team, got that?"

"Got it." She smiled. "I should probably get Mee-Maw home. I know she has to be exhausted."

"Good idea. Oh, and good news." He smiled. "I'm going to have some free time tomorrow. Can I take you out?"

"Absolutely." She leaned up and kissed him again,

with a lot more passion than he might have wanted on display in the middle of the police station, but she didn't care. For a few moments in the truck, she'd believed she would never celebrate another Valentine's Day with him, never spend another day with him, and she didn't want to pass up a single opportunity to kiss him.

On the way to Freely Lakes, Charlotte's phone wouldn't stop buzzing.

"Mee-Maw, what's that about?" Ally glanced over at her.

"It's Jeff." She sighed and stared down at the phone. "I guess he heard about everything. I told him I'm fine, but he keeps asking questions."

"That's sweet of him. Are you going to see him tonight?"

"I'm tired. I'm not sure about that." She shrugged.

"Do you want me to stay with you?" Ally pulled into Freely Lakes and parked near the entrance.

"No, it's all right. Take the car tonight, and pick me up in the morning."

"Okay, Mee-Maw."

"Good night, Ally." She kissed her cheek. "I love you so much."

"I love you, too, Mee-Maw."

Charlotte stepped out of the car and headed

inside. Her entire body was heavy and achy from rolling around in the truck. All she wanted to do was lay down. However, once she did she couldn't sleep. Her restless mind kept returning to the day. Finally, a few minutes before midnight, she texted Jeff.

I can't sleep.

A moment later, he texted back.

Be there in two minutes.

She smiled at the thought, and suddenly it struck her that she didn't just want a friend to come comfort her. She wanted Jeff. The thought of seeing him made her heart flutter. She was already far more involved than she intended.

When she answered the door, Jeff hugged her, then stood back to take a good look at her.

"Charlotte." He brushed his palm along the curve of her cheek and studied her. His eyes were anxious, as if he didn't quite believe that she was there. "Are you hurt?"

"No." She smiled some as the warmth of his touch soothed her nerves. "Not really. Just so glad to be free. I'm sorry, I guess all of this must have ruined your plans for Valentine's Day. I'm not sure I'll have enough energy for everything you had planned."

"Yes, it's true." He gazed into her eyes. "I had a lot of plans for tomorrow night. Maybe too many. But all I really want is to take another walk under the stars with you."

"Me too." She sighed as she leaned against his chest. It didn't matter what she called him, or whether he wanted things to become more serious. The only thing that mattered was that his arms were around her, warm and strong, and not asking for anything more than her presence.

"Happy Valentine's Day, Charlotte." He kissed the top of her head.

"Happy Valentine's Day to you, too, Jeff." She turned her head up enough to meet his lips for a soft kiss.

The End

HOT CHOCOLATE CUPCAKE RECIPE

INGREDIENTS:

Cupcakes:

1 teaspoon baking powder

1 1/4 cups all-purpose flour

1/4 cup unsweetened cocoa powder

5 1/2 ounces butter

1 cup light brown sugar

3/4 cup milk

2 eggs at room temperature

Chocolate Frosting:

1 cup confectioners' sugar

2 tablespoons unsweetened cocoa powder
2 1/4 ounces butter, softened
2 tablespoons milk
Mini-marshmallows for decorating

PREPARATION:

Preheat the oven to 350 degrees Fahrenheit.

Line a 12-hole muffin pan with cupcake liners.

Sift the baking powder and flour into a bowl. Sift the cocoa powder into another bowl.

Melt the butter, brown sugar and milk together in a double boiler. Whisk in the cocoa powder until combined. Leave aside to cool slightly.

Whisk the eggs into the milk mixture.

Gradually add the baking powder and flour into the milk mixture and mix until combined.

Pour the mixture into a jug and divide between the cupcake liners.

Bake for 15-20 minutes or until a skewer inserted into the middle comes out clean.

Leave in the pan for 10 minutes to cool.

Remove from the pan and cool completely on a cooling rack.

To make the chocolate frosting. Sift the confectioners' sugar and cocoa powder into a bowl.

In another bowl cream the butter, milk and half the cocoa powder and confectioners' sugar.

When combined add the rest of the sugar mixture and mix together until smooth.

Smooth the frosting over the cupcakes with the back of a spoon.

Decorate with mini-marshmallows.

Enjoy!

ALSO BY CINDY BELL

Pageant and Poison

Conditioner and a Corpse

Mistletoe, Makeup and Murder

Hairpin, Hair Dryer and Homicide

Blush, a Bride and a Body

Shampoo and a Stiff

Cosmetics, a Cruise and a Killer

Lipstick, a Long Iron and Lifeless

Camping, Concealer and Criminals

Treated and Dyed

A Wrinkle-Free Murder

SAGE GARDENS COZY MYSTERIES

Birthdays Can Be Deadly

Money Can Be Deadly

Trust Can Be Deadly

Ties Can Be Deadly

Rocks Can Be Deadly

Jewelry Can Be Deadly

Numbers Can Be Deadly

Memories Can Be Deadly

Paintings Can Be Deadly

Snow Can Be Deadly

Tea Can Be Deadly

A MACARON PATISSERIE COZY MYSTERY SERIES

Sifting for Suspects

Recipes and Revenge

Mansions, Macarons and Murder

NUTS ABOUT NUTS COZY MYSTERIES

A Tough Case to Crack

A Seed of Doubt

HEAVENLY HIGHLAND INN COZY MYSTERIES

Murdering the Roses

Dead in the Daisies

Killing the Carnations

Drowning the Daffodils

Suffocating the Sunflowers

Books, Bullets and Blooms

A Deadly Serious Gardening Contest

A Bridal Bouquet and a Body

Digging for Dirt

CHOCOLATE CENTERED COZY MYSTERIES

The Sweet Smell of Murder

A Deadly Delicious Delivery

A Bitter Sweet Murder

A Treacherous Tasty Trail

Luscious Pastry at a Lethal Party

Trouble and Treats

Fudge Films and Felonies

Custom-Made Murder

Skydiving, Soufflés and Sabotage

WENDY THE WEDDING PLANNER COZY
MYSTERIES

Matrimony, Money and Murder

Chefs, Ceremonies and Crimes

Knives and Nuptials

Mice, Marriage and Murder

ABOUT THE AUTHOR

Cindy Bell is the author of the cozy mystery series Donut Truck, Dune House, Sage Gardens, Chocolate Centered, Macaron Patisserie, Nuts about Nuts, Bekki the Beautician, Heavenly Highland Inn and Wendy the Wedding Planner.

Cindy has always loved reading, but it is only recently that she has discovered her passion for writing romantic cozy mysteries. She loves walking along the beach thinking of the next adventure her characters can embark on.

You can sign up for her newsletter so you are notified of her latest releases at http://www.cindybellbooks.com.

Printed in Great Britain
by Amazon